MW00834922

STILL
LIFE
WITH
MEREDITH

ANN
LEWINSON

Outpost19 | San Francisco
outpost19.com

Copyright 2020 by Ann Lewinson
Published 2020 by Outpost19
All rights reserved.

Lewinson, Ann
Still Life with Meredith/ Ann Lewinson
ISBN 978-1-944853-69-3 (pbk)

Library of Congress Control Number: pending

UNCORRECTED PROOF

This is an advance copy. Corrections to the text
and cover will be incorporated for the final
printing.

ISBN: 978-1-944853-69-3
Pub date: 4/7/2020
104 pages $10.00 paperback

Promotions:
galley mailing to mainstream and literary reviewers;
New York/regional author events;
related essays and interviews placed near pub date;
ongoing social media

Contact: Jon Roemer jon@outpost19.com

Thank you for your interest in Ann Lewinson's
STILL LIFE WITH MEREDITH.

Here's our jacket copy:

Behind the glass windows of a storefront-turned-
apartment, an art handler at a contemporary art
museum sits among dead birds awaiting the return of
her roommate, an emerging artist of growing notoriety.
While she waits, she ransacks her past while discours-
ing on Dutch still life painting, the mating habits of her
species and others, and the extreme measures taken by
the French psychoanalyst Marie Bonaparte to achieve
sexual fulfillment.

This audacious burning match of a novella marks the
debut of a writer of uncommon insight, boundless
curiosity and mordant wit, whose jaundiced eye takes on
the comic excesses of contemporary art and the multi-
fariousness of bad sex in equal measure. Masterful in its
breadth—at once funny, shocking and erudite—STILL
LIFE WITH MEREDITH contemplates the thin line
that separates sanity from madness in a world that has a
hard time telling the difference.

Ann Lewinson's fiction has appeared in *Agni, Hayden's
Ferry Review,* MoMA PS1's Special Projects Writers'
Series and other places. A 2014 fellow at the Edward
F. Albee Foundation, she is also a playwright, journalist
and film critic who has reviewed movies for *ARTnews,
The Boston Phoenix, The Hartford Advocate* and *The Kansas
City Star.* She lives in New York.

Advance Praise

"Hovering somewhere between Nell Zink and David Markson, STILL LIFE WITH MEREDITH is an arrow pulled back in the bow. It's as funny as it is sinister, filled up with facts that stretch the fiction beyond recognition. Take the afternoon off and marvel at this new shape for narrative."
— Jac Jemc, author of *False Bingo* and *The Grip of It*

"If Tom Robbins and Dostoevsky had a art feminist historian baby who suckled esoterica from an ancient wet nurse sorceress, she'd probably sound a lot like the narrator of STILL LIFE WITH MEREDITH. Part curio cabinet, part macabre romp, this is a story about spectacle, pleasure, friendship and the body that gets all the way under the skin. Lewinson is an electric new voice whose prose cuts like a scalpel."
— Kristen Iskandrian, author of *Motherest*

"STILL LIFE WITH MEREDITH is a guided tour of a museum of perverse fascinations: wandering clitorises, divine foreskins, animal abuse, and the princess/psychoanalyst Marie Bonaparte. It's funny and fearlessly weird, with moments of jarring profundity and long stretches of delicious brilliance. Lewinson is a more profane and pitiless Renata Adler, and her novella is the most decadently imaginative thing I've read in years."
— Sandra Newman, author of *The Heavens* and *The Country of Ice Cream Star*

We hope you enjoy it!

For Marie Bonaparte,
who deserved better

STILL
LIFE
WITH
MEREDITH

Marie Bonaparte had her clitoris moved three times.

The first time in 1927 in Vienna, under the surgical knife of one Dr. Halban, who was reputed to have performed sex changes on men. All the ransacking of her childhood on the couch of her mentor Sigmund Freud had not cured Marie's frigidity, and so the French psychoanalyst, Greek princess and last of the Bonapartes had determined that her problems were anatomical, theorizing that tall women such as herself had too great a distance between their clitoris and vagina.

"Shared pleasure between lovers exists only in novels," wrote Bonaparte. In *Madame Bovary*, in *Anna Karenina*, in *Camille*. Not in the nonfictive marital bed, or the adulterous bed, and Marie had attempted in both. Five women had been cured under Dr. Halban's scalpel. She would be next.

Thus, the operation. This wasn't a simple tuck of skin, you see. Halban sliced the clitoris clear off, sewing it closer to the urethra, like a button. Twenty-two minutes. Local anesthesia. Her friend Ruth Mack watched. Perhaps took notes. Held her hand.

Two years later, the first operation having failed to lift her sexual malaise, Marie returned to Dr. Halban's operating table. This time he threw in a hysterectomy, indicated by the patient's perennially inflamed fallopian tubes. Ruth Mack present, again. In 1931, Dr. Halban moved Marie's clitoris one more time, to no avail. As she lay in bed, Marie marveled that the spot from which her clitoris had initially been severed remained sensitive to the touch.

That Marie's husband, Prince George of Greece, preferred the company of his Uncle Waldemar, that her son was in analysis with her lover Dr. Rudolph Loewenstein, that she and her son openly discussed their mutual incestuous longings, that it took her seemingly forever to undress in front of longtime paramour and eleven-time French Prime Minister Aristide Briand, that she desperately tried to recover her love letters to him before the 1929 operation, that Dr. Freud thought it was a terrible idea, that when she was a baby she watched her wet nurse rutting with the stable boy through a fog of opium — all of this should have given someone pause.

It gives me pause. In my darkened lair, in the midst of a pause suspended in time. I have paused. I am pausing. I continue to pause.

If you think my lair is dark because I live in some Dostoyevskian-Ellisonian basement, you are mistaken. I live above ground, in a storefront, Meredith's storefront — I guess it's my storefront now — darkened, by me. I've painted the windows black. She kept birds in the windows that would fly through the room as if it were an uncaged pet store. Now they litter the rusty orange carpet, canaries in the proverbial coal mine.

I could not live as Meredith did, inhabiting a human terrarium with all the world looking in. She'd make fun of me for hanging my clothes right outside the shower so I could grab them with one naked, wet arm and change in the stall. But one naked, wet arm was all I would add to the avian frolics that attracted passersby. That and the spectacle of two young women living in a storefront, one of whom could care less whether strangers were watching her getting dressed. Or cared very much. It's really the same thing.

Since Meredith left to rendezvous in the Brazilian rainforest with some once-and-future boyfriend — she invited me along, but the third wheel always gets derailed — I've been redecorating, piling up books, trying to expunge Meredith's traces from the storefront. Which is difficult, since she found the place, installed the toilet, shower, stove, did all the plumbing and wiring. I could never do that, wouldn't know where to begin — it wouldn't even have occurred to me to hunt down the landlord of a vacant storefront in an iffy neighborhood. I admire Meredith's initiative. No, I hate Meredith's initiative. Again, it's the same thing.

I can still see the tracks on the carpet where she parked her motorcycle. I have shampooed and scrubbed on my hands and knees, but the tracks won't fade.

After painting the windows black, I began dismantling Meredith's sculptures, one by one. I was just going to drag them out to the dumpster, but when I found myself taking one apart to get it through the door — a hulking metal monstrosity she called a postmodern *Gates of Hell,* a labored cry of anguish by someone who wouldn't know anguish if it resectioned her clitoris three times — the act of dismembering took on its own discrete pleasure, and I ended up sitting there for weeks, taking apart every single one of Meredith's sculptures, reducing them to their elements, and the elements to the garbage.

•

I have not left this room for longer than I care to reveal to you. I have found that isolation breeds productivity, and I'm reluctant to mess with that.

Here is what I do with my time:

1. Write this book. If you're reading this in some sort of published form — which is a laughable prospect — know that it has consumed more hungry days and sleepless nights than anyone should ever devote to any single, meaningless task, that it was written on yellow legal pads with black Flair pens — I only write on yellow legal pads with black Flair pens — that I have been writing this book for so long, have subjected it to so many revisions, that gray has begun to sneak into my uncut hair and lines are creasing around my pallid eyes, even though they seldom see the sun. That is to say, I hope you appreciate the effort.

2. Read books on three topics: psychoanalysis, anthropology, and natural history. I no longer read novels — I can't find my place in the world of male novelists who churn out vast, conspiracy-driven Americas in which women make only fleeting appearances as seductive ciphers, and if I read one more novel about three generations of ethnic women sewing a quilt I'll just kill myself, literally, in some theatrical, symbolic manner, maybe plunge a knitting needle between my breasts. Anyway, novels are a waste of time. You only have so much time on this planet to learn things.

3. Sit in the far-left corner of this storefront on the floor, knees scrunched up to my chest, picking at the wall-to-wall carpet.

Of course, I do a few other things. I take all my nourishment in liquid form, processing my strict vegan diet through an old Acme juicer with a knob of ginger here and a clove of garlic there. I stand on my head for fifteen minutes a day. It doesn't hurt as much as you think. After a while you don't feel any pressure. In fact, you don't feel anything at all.

It wasn't always like this. I used to have a job at the contemporary art museum on the waterfront, the one they built on that decommissioned aircraft carrier, the one that's always getting picketed by veterans or Christians or feminists or just regular folk who object to penis-nosed child mannequins shoving their heads up each other's asses while wearing Nikes.

I was the chief animal wrangler — usually the only animal wrangler. I used to feed the fish in Nam June Paik's forty fish tanks in front of forty televisions showing Merce Cunningham dancing a *pas de deux* with his Winky-Dinky electronic doppelganger. I scooped up after Jannis Kounellis' twelve horses, hitched to the walls of the museum. And when Joseph Beuys spent a week fenced in with a coyote to heal our nation's original sin through a confrontation with its spirit animal, I cannot begin to tell you what a pain in the ass he was. Worse than the coyote.

I found a certain deep resonance in this animal wrangler job — there was an honesty about the art for whose upkeep I was responsible, a directness, an absence of mediation in an overmediated world. It brought art back to its naked origins, those 15,000-year-old cave paintings in Lascaux, animals painted with their own blood.

And yet the sorry truth is that I harbor no particular affection for animals. Mild indifference is more like it. When I was a kid I had fish, but they always ended up floating dead on top if they weren't shitting long ribbons down to the bottom of the tank. Actually, that was kind of cool, watching those long ribbons of shit, awaiting the moment of detachment.

Detachment. I was eight years old, maybe, stomping down the ramp at the Guggenheim, enchanted by the echo of my little feet, when I was halted midway by Robert Rauschenberg's *Monogram* — the Angora goat with paint on its snout, stuffed with sawdust and stuffed in a tire. I tugged at my parents and pointed. My parents tugged me onward. They told me that wasn't art; here, look at this Picasso of dismembered women.

Okay, they really didn't say that last part, but I'm trying, in my heavy-handed way, to point out some irony. That goat, looking so helpless, objectified, snuffed and stuffed, once alive, now reduced to medium and metaphor. Yes, I have little affection for animals, but I couldn't take my eyes off this one. Something horrific had been done to this goat and it turned me on, to the extent that an eight-year-old can be turned on. The next day I was in the garage on all fours, a spare tire around my neck, wishing someone would take a picture.

I haven't touched a speck of meat since.

That said, I have no respect for your garden-variety vegetarian. Vegetarianism is a luxury of urban life — we who are estranged from the land, who cannot understand how Farmer Bob can love Clarabelle Cow and then feast on her back when her milk runs dry. How the coyote kills the fox who kills the squirrel. We have the luxury of romanticizing animals because we're not dependent on them for survival.

Instead, we keep them as pets. Pet-lovers (and I use the term sarcastically, for what kind of lover keeps their beloved locked inside all day, away from fresh air and others of its kind, feeds their beloved crap not fit for consumption by "higher" species, hacks off their beloved's genitals, for chrissake) treat you like some anti-American freak when you recoil from their affectionate pooch, but I'm not alone in my loathing. I submit a work by Marco Evaristti, who installed ten blenders holding ten goldfish in the museum and invited visitors to hit the button. Two got Osterized at the opening party, and five of the remaining fish hit the blades before PETA made us pull the plugs.

I will admit that one of those five was done in by me. I had to put on a ridiculous disguise to do it — wig, hat, glasses, fake nose — because if I'd done it after hours I would not have had the witnesses that such an act requires.

I cannot convey strongly enough the cathartic power of pulverizing a goldfish. Pushing that button, seeing that golden whirl — it was like offering up an ancient sacrifice, and wouldn't the world be more peaceful if we brought back burnt offerings and on weekends offered up a goat to the gods? It would really bring people together. I read once that Abraham's binding of Isaac wasn't so farfetched because in ancient times people would routinely sacrifice their kids for a good harvest, but I don't believe it for a minute. Child sacrifice is part of so many ancient myths because it's a forbidden desire, the lonely kid standing in for the lonely kid. *Had Gad-ya-a-a-ah Had Gadya.* It's all about death, you see, I see, sitting among these dead birds, Meredith's dead birds, flat on their backs, their little feet erect. I really should sweep them up, throw them out, or dress them in little sweaters like Annette Messager's sparrows in the Pompidou. They will start to smell soon, if they haven't already. You should tell me if it smells in here — I'm not sure I haven't gotten used to it.

Most of the animals in the museum are dead, of course — most famously Damien Hirst's *Some Comfort Gained from the Acceptance of the Inherent Lies in Everything,* which you might be more familiar with as the dead cow sliced into a dozen pieces. I used to spend hours wandering around that thing, sandwiching myself between the Plexiglas cases and examining those circular innards, like tree-trunk rings, ancient and unfathomable.

We had Jordan Baseman's skinned cat and dog hanging on the wall, and enough stuffed animals to keep a taxidermist in business for years. Mark Dion's animal lynching: a cat, snake, frog, lizard, a couple of birds, tarred and feathered and hanging from a tree. Paul McCarthy's motorized father nodding while his mannequin son dry-humps a goat. (Talk about ancient taboos.) Thomas Grünfeld's dog with a sheep's head — a sheepdog, get it? It's sad when they stoop to lame-ass puns. That's one I'd do, if I did that sort of thing — a lame ass. I'd just break a donkey's legs, stick him in a pen. Ha-ha.

Every morning, before the museum opened, I would clean out the dead flies sealed inside the glass with Hirst's severed cow's head and pour fresh ones in. I know you're thinking, *Gross, you had to smell that decomposing flesh*, but it was such a scam. You were supposed to think the flies were dining on USDA-grade beef, but it was so fake — under that cow hair and teeth, there was nothing but chicken wire. Chicken wire!

Sometimes the flies would make it through the glass, and visitors might get a nip or two, a souvenir welt they could show off at the office on Monday — *Guess where I was this weekend? Those picketers threw elephant dung at me!* Of course, refreshing the box with fresh flies every day, I got bitten a lot. First I started to feel a little flu-ish, with a runny nose and an achy head that wouldn't go away, but then I started forgetting things, and remembering things that people told me never happened. I had headaches for days at a time. My vision would blur. I'd hear echoes, or sounds from far away. Sometimes I couldn't see anything for the surges of ether before me, couldn't hear anything for the din of molecules mixing and combining. The noise was unbearable.

The doctors didn't know what was wrong with me. The museum discharged me, and now I collect disability. The juice, the head-standing, it's all part of my own treatment — I think it calms my worst symptoms, allows me to push through the muck in my brain, the sensory overload.

My disease has focused me, made sense of my time on earth. I no longer waste time having "fun." I was not always so frugal. I had Meredith. I had men. Lots of men. One interchangeable widget after another.

•

For a while there, I was lurching towards promiscuity.

A joyless, mechanical promiscuity, accepting whatever invitations came my way. I'd close my eyes — not to hide from their lust, but to hide my lack of it from them. I'd hold my breath so as not to smell the sweat that desire, if I'd had any, would have deodorized. I collected mementos — ticket stubs, tollbooth receipts, museum maps, postcards — and filed them in alphabetized accordion folders tied with brown ribbon. It's important to keep good records.

My maximum was three months, but I rarely made it to two. Frequent turnover is essential when you're trying to be a sexual adventuress. The object was to experience as many bodies as possible — the obese and the anorexic, the poky flesh of the middle-aged and the wiry bones of the drug-addled, the rich boys who had burned out their dicks with coke, the working-class boys who lived in their parents' basements but were muscular machines in bed.

Marie Bonaparte writes: "Male sexuality is thus centrifugal, convex in its orientation, while that of the female sexuality is centripetal and concave." I don't get the centrifugal-centripetal part, but convex, yes. I did want to fuck like a man.

I never said no. I was just so flattered to be asked. Women like Meredith, they never understand.

•

I met Meredith in the museum one disastrous Saturday afternoon, after an accident in the emerging artists wing during the carnival show. You must have read about it. The museum had commissioned some recent graduates to resituate the nineteenth-century notion of the carnival (not the carnivalesque, which is an entirely different thing) within our post-wonder era. I'm not too clear on the details, but I can dig up the call for entries if you're interested.

Anyway, it was one of those relational aesthetics things. One artist constructed a funhouse with distorted mirrors that was supposed to make a rather obvious point about eating disorders. Another built a "Dunk the Mayor" booth to protest the mayor's pledge to cut funding for the museum, I think over those penis-nosed child mannequins. Some luckless sap had to sit on a perch in the booth, half-filled with water, wearing an Easter Island-size paper-maché mayor-mask, waiting for someone to throw a ball at the target with enough force to flush him into the drink. There was a flea circus in a sealed fish tank outfitted with tiny trapezes and trampolines. Circles of magnifying glass were affixed to the sides of the tank like portholes for close-ups of the acrobatics, but the fleas just buzzed around. A large terrarium held what purported to be a secret glimpse of an alien civilization, but it was really just an ant farm. At the center of all this was a small Ferris wheel — one passenger at a time, please, you must be under 5' 5" and 120 pounds to enjoy this ride — made entirely of recycled metal, with a seat of Coke cans that crunched when you sat on them. Every afternoon at two there was a freak show, in which heavily tattooed musicians hammered nails into uncomfortable places.

I don't think you'll be surprised when I tell you what happened. It was about a quarter-past two, the freaks were halfway through their show. Metal Man, so called for the hunks of metal poking through his face and chest as well as, one assumes, less visible parts of his body, was to lift a set of fifty-pound barbells hooked to the two-foot-long metal rod that bisected his nostrils. This required an impressive backbend, and the gallery was so quiet you could hear the ants farming. The barbells went up in the air. The room held its breath.

It was at this moment that some kid thought it would be hilarious to take the ball from the mayor-dunker and toss it at Metal Man, in what were presumed to be his heavily armed nether regions. What followed was a chain of reactions worthy of Rube Goldberg. The ball hit the balls. Metal Man doubled over as the barbells fell, along with the two-foot-long rod and attached bits of nose, all of which rolled into the funhouse mirrors so fast that they shattered, a shard of mirror flying into the dunking booth and the exposed eye of the mayor, who plummeted straight into the water, banging his head so hard on the glass that the booth smashed, flooding the gallery and nearly electrocuting the woman sitting on the stalled Ferris wheel, who was propelled with the force of the shock smack into the ant farm. Only the fleas remained unscathed.

It was my job to recover the ants, at least the ones that hadn't drowned.

"Okay if I hit the power?"

I had been watching her towel off her Ferris wheel, as if the afternoon's calamity had been no big deal. She walked past me, sodden on the floor, almost imperious. I marveled at the way her jeans fit, like a boy's, low on her hips, tight against her thighs. I wanted to touch those thighs. No, I wanted to have those thighs. On *my* body. I buried that familiar intermingling of envy and lust. She would not see me coveting her thighs.

"This yours?"

She was speaking to me. She of the perfect thighs. Thighs that would pass the Eileen Ford Leg Test — I may seem to be above such things, but I will not pretend that I have never opened a fashion magazine, and so I not only know who Eileen Ford was but the substance of her famous Leg Test. It's like a Leonardo diagram defining the correct proportions. The legs, when pressed together, must form three diamonds — between the thighs, between the knee and upper calf muscle, and between the upper calf muscle and ankle. And I found myself possessed with the alarming desire to perform the Eileen Ford Test on the legs before me, to measure the width of the diamond between her thighs, the diamond that I knew was there, obscured by those jeans that I would unbutton so that I could rest my cheek against that pale diamond, unbuttoned right there, sopping wet on the floor among the dead ants and fish and broken glass. The temptation was too great. I couldn't bear to look up above her paint-speckled Converse hi-tops. "No, I just work here," I said. "Animal Wrangler."

"You must be busy these days."

"We're doing an all-animal show in the spring."

"You take care of the dead ones too?"

"Sometimes. Not much to wrangle, though."

"I was thinking of doing something with road kill. I use recycled materials, mostly metal, and there are a lot of dead animals out there on the highway, just decomposing. No one buries them. They just lie there, waiting to be eaten by other animals. And how do they get to be road kill? By unlucky collisions with big hunks of metal. And I've been using a lot of auto parts lately…."

I nodded, still on the floor, coaxing the ants into a glass jar. She never looked down at me as she talked. She was used to being listened to by strangers, to being found fascinating. But then a business card fluttered down to me. "I'm having a party tomorrow night. You should come."

Her storefront was near the university, right on the park — this was when nobody went into the park, before the gentry moved in and renovated the brownstones, before those free-range bistros and wooden toy stores and single-origin coffee joints, and the neighborhood held that eerie nighttime quiet engendered by fear. But her lights were on — Christmas lights, framing the windows of a store that sold nothing.

Branches had been set up in the windows, and birds flew from perch to perch. The room was dense with people from somewhere else who all seemed to know each other. People and their smoke. No one noticed me. Ban smoking all you want, but it will always be the lingua franca of the people who matter. Without a cigarette between your fingers you disappear.

I wandered invisible through the crowd. Some of the freaks were there. Metal Man had a large bandage on his stitched-up nose that made him sound like he had a cold.

On one wall were large-format black-and-white photographs of a naked woman of indeterminable ethnicity, impossibly glamorous, impeccably formed.

Beneath them was a battered yellow sofa with an undulating, carved wooden back, the kind of Salvation Army special people like Meredith always have; beside it a mannequin's head impaled on a metal frame a little taller than my own, breast implants hanging at chest level. I had never seen breast implants up close, and summoned the nerve to poke them. They felt like sacks of oil.

"You like Meredith's work?" A man was standing beside me, older than most of the people there. He introduced himself as Meredith's roommate, the photographer of those pictures on the wall.

I kept poking.

"They used to be inside her," he said, nodding at the model in the photographs. I shuddered and withdrew my hand, looking for something to wipe it on.

I leaned against a wall sipping a room-temperature beer and observing, like an anthropologist. On the rare occasion that someone invites me to a party I always end up playing Margaret Mead. I don't enter the bush that way, it's just that once I'm there it's like they're all speaking Swahili. I fall back on old habits, observing the mating rituals of this foreign, blithely self-confident race. Will Red Polka Dot Dress and Bettie Page Hairdo go home with Greasy Hair Holey T-shirt and Plumber's Ass or Thinks He's the Millionth Coming of Jim Morrison but is Closer to Jesus in a Community Theater Production of *Godspell?*

This usually keeps me occupied for hours, but that night I was overcome with a more pressing desire: I wanted to figure out how to stay in this storefront on the park with its orange wall-to-wall carpet and uncaged birds. How to not leave the party.

•

"She just stayed."

Matt is looking at the clouded sky, not at me. I had asked him how he'd met his live-in girlfriend, whose side of the mattress I'd taken while she was in Prague. I always wanted to know how the men I was sleeping with met their girlfriends, their wives.

"I had a party. She was there, with a friend. They got pretty high and started fighting over me."

I try to imagine two women fighting over Matt — concave, bespectacled Matt, his skin a canvas of pockmarks, a man so disengaged from sex he can take a swig of beer without breaking rhythm. He never comes.

"A real cat fight, trying to scratch each other's eyes out. One of them came after the other with a broken beer bottle. Really shut down the party. And then the three of us just went to bed."

Huh.

"In the morning the girls had another fight, and she won. So she stayed."

"It's been a couple years?"

"Three and a half."

Three and a half. I wanted to lie on Meredith's mattress while she was in Prague and tell some guy how there was this party, and I never went home.

Matt and I are lying on folding chairs behind a rundown motel, watching the lightning across the lake. We're drinking beers he's wheedled out of the proprietor, who greeted us in his undershirt with a Bud in his hand and several more on his breath. It's late, and Matt had despaired of finding an open store. This is not thirst, but the anxiety of someone who cannot fall asleep without a two-drink minimum.

We have been driving around the perimeter of the lake, one of the Great ones. The trip was Matt's idea; I just invited myself along. He seemed baffled — we barely knew each other — and all day, from the diner over-easies to the presidential homestead to the Potawatomi craft market in a shuttered mall's parking lot, we have avoided speaking about the previous night, in a better place than this.

That first night I lay on the king-size bed in wait, listening as he brushed his teeth, taking in the room's must of discomfort and sleaze. The desk clerk had tried to upsell us to the honeymoon suite, with a vibrating bed and a heart-shaped Jacuzzi, unaware of our mutual embarrassment and subterfuge. When his teeth were clean Matt climbed on top of me as if performing a duty, joylessly. "Jeux" from Debussy's *Daphnis and Chloë* was playing on the radio, too high-spirited for the occasion. Unable to find the off-button in the dark, he ripped the radio out of its socket and hurled it across the room.

During the day it's like we're distant cousins with little in common. The trip keeps us occupied — the historical sites, the tourist traps, the search for what Matt calls authentic frozen custard but to me is just soft ice cream. Custard, he explains, has eggs in it. I'm not sure I want eggs in my ice cream.

At night we replay our simulacrum of lust. I try to kiss him, out of some felt obligation, but he turns his head.

After we return home and I have dutifully filed the ticket stubs, the blurry receipts, the clearcut motel matchbooks, he visits me a few times. He likes having sex on furniture. The kitchen table, the desk, chairs. The acrobatics and hour-long screws seem to compensate for an ending determined only by exhaustion and boredom. I never ask why the condoms are empty.

Meredith, I am certain, has never seen a condom emerge empty. If she's into that sort of thing. She is locked in the center of a room of admirers, embracing one, catching a light from another. There's a Peggy Lee song running through my head: "I know a little bit about a lot of things/But I don't know enough about you."

•

"I catch the disease that I study," wrote Montaigne, and so do I.

Montaigne recounts the strange case of Marie Germain of Vitry-le-François, a 22-year-old woman who pulled a muscle while jumping, causing a penis and scrotum to spring from her crotch. "Among the girls there," writes Montaigne, "a song is still current by which they warn each other not to take big strides for fear of becoming boys, like Marie Germain."

I took Montaigne's collected essays very seriously in college, highlighting passages I thought profound, a practice I curse now, leafing through the hefty paperback — I can only see the highlighted text, the rest recedes into unimportance, and I am beholden to my youthful judgments. To me now, Montaigne is just a canonized *News of the Weird:* "French Babe Pole Vaults into Frenchman!" Today Montaigne would be churning out click-bait on a content farm in Hyderabad.

I am 15 and striding like Marie Germain down my high school hallway in my new Frye boots. Just like Linda Ronstadt, I think. "You take large steps," some girl says. I am so proud of my new Frye boots, I want to see them way out in front, so that I can admire them without looking down. I thrust each leg as far as it will go, like that "Keep on truckin'" guy.

I didn't know that if you took large strides you'd turn into a boy. Now that I think about it, it happens all the time — metaphorically, that is. And perhaps I *was* trying.

Miss Mollycoddle's Family Living class, sixth grade: After five years of coed visits from Miss Mollycoddle, with her pictures of happy gorilla families and happy bunny families, we are suddenly segregated, the boys exiled to the playground. We're assigned to cover a shoebox with wrapping paper and fill it with Midol and sanitary napkins and tampons in a variety of thicknesses. This will be our "menstrual emergency kit." You will soon become women and bleed and have terrible pain every month, she warns us, and it's important to be prepared. I imagine all the blood in my body draining in a ferocious flood that I will try to dam in vain with these napkins and cardboard tubes, when I'm not doubling over with excruciating cramps.

Every morning the Orthodox Jew thanks God that he was not born a woman. The Orthodox Jew is onto something.

•

It's hard to make plans with Meredith right now. She's going to fill a clear plastic life-size replica of her body with her own menstrual blood. She's got her work cut out for her. She spends practically one week a month squatting over a child's plastic training potty. When she must go out, she uses a tampon and wrings it out into a glass jar she keeps in the refrigerator. When the jar fills up it goes into the freezer. I've offered her my diaphragm to collect her blood when she goes out — they haven't yet come out with those menstrual cups — but she says that's too easy. It's the effort — the squatting, the wringing — that makes it art.

The menstrual cycles of women who live together are supposed to sync up, but so far that hasn't happened. I continue to get my period on the fourteenth of every month, even thirty-day months and February. Every bloody Valentine's Day.

Meredith menstruates without symbolic baggage. She's been working with menstrual blood for a while now, dipping lacy white lingerie into it, smearing it on naked Barbie dolls. It's in response to the tradition of painting being a man's art, she says; this paint is wholly hers. I suspect she also gets off on the smell of her personal funk.

It fascinates me, this blood. Its goopiness, its dark balls of clot, its stringy strands bodied with pus. Its bright redness at onset and final dregs of brown. I had never seen someone else's menstrual blood before. Once or twice, maybe, a dried tampon that missed a public toilet. An unwrapped napkin in a stall's disposal bin. It wasn't like the revolting sight of someone else's shit in an unflushed bowl, gagging on the smell. It was oddly familiar, and comforting — she is like me, under her different skin and hair and clothes and life. We have this one thing in common.

In Sweden they have these feminine hygiene disposal bins, freestanding and tall as garbage cans. When you open the bin you don't see the contents, just like the book return at the public library. The label says this is "ultra-hygienic." But I feel sorry for Swedish women, missing out on a brief, forced instance of bonding. With their suicide rate the Swedes need all the connection they can get. Hygiene isn't everything, you know.

•

I am sitting in a restaurant, waiting for Meredith. It's a family restaurant on the highway, an old one, not a chain, with dark wood paneling and maroon upholstery and pictures of cows on the walls. The waitress comes over to the table and picks up one of the menus she'd put down not a moment before. She's sorry, but it hasn't been stapled, she says. She leans over, right next to me, and aims a staple gun at the cardboard. The staples fly into my face. I go into the restroom and pull tiny staples out of my skin.

This is probably a dream.

•

An invitation to Mary Cat McAllister's sleepover party represents my social triumph, as far as I'm concerned. That Mary Cat's mother made her daughter invite every girl in her sixth-grade class, not only the charismatic and glossy-haired, does not matter. The fact is I'm here, in Mary Cat's pink-flowered bedroom, kneeling on the carpet in my floor-length granny gown patterned with little red strawberries and trimmed with lace, my favorite nightgown ever until this very moment among the simpler flannels of my classmates, and I wish I'd worn something else. We are eating the s'mores we've just made in the McAllisters' yellow-ruffled kitchen. I learned in Girl Scouts that the only way to really make s'mores is to toast the marshmallows over a smoldering campfire, but the McAllisters' toaster oven will do, since it's February and Mary Cat says so.

Everyone wants to be your friend when your name is Mary Cat. Not even the teachers call her Mary Catherine — Mr. Marsh attacks that Cat with a hard *K*, like she's special, Miss Mary Cat-Cat-Cat all dressed in black-black-black with silver buttons-buttons-buttons down her back-back-back. If my name were Mary Cat I'd jump so high-high-high I'd never come back-back-back 'til the Fourth of July-ly-ly.

We've been regressing from impending puberty, playing with Mary Cat's old Barbies, a naked pile of twisted necks and mussy hair. Mary Cat has decided that her formerly Leisure Suit Ken is Mr. Marsh, and another girl is slamming him on top of Malibu Barbie. "Look, it's Mr. Marsh and Miss Mollycoddle," she says. We giggle.

Except for one girl, who looks bored. She doesn't know who these teachers are, doesn't go to our school. But Mary Cat has told us all about her: Meredith goes to Sutton Academy. She's rich. She lives on the other side of town and keeps a pony in her backyard. Her parents have a heated driveway that melts snow the second it touches. They even have heated towel racks in the bathroom. It occurs to me that this Meredith would eclipse even Mary Cat if she deigned to attend public school. And Meredith does indeed take over the evening.

She proposes a game. We put all the Barbies in a pile, close our eyes, and grab one. If two girls lay their hands on the same Barbie, which is inevitable since there are eight of them and nine of us, they have to go into the closet.

The purpose of this game is a little beyond me, but I still don't want to play. Each time two girls go into the closet everyone else hoots "Woo-woo" because they've done this before, at all those other sixth-grade slumber parties I wasn't invited to because the other mothers weren't as considerate as Mrs. McAllister. Meredith times them — two minutes, she says, is enough. They emerge, triumphant or blushing, to another chorus of "woo-woo"'s. I have no idea what they do in that closet. I am determined not to find out.

I try to relax my eyelids, shuttering only three-quarters of the way so I can see who's grabbing which doll, but someone catches me at it, and from then on I scrunch my eyes up tight and exaggerated. It doesn't occur to me to wonder how I was caught with my eyes at quarter-mast.

I release my grip on a Barbie the second I feel someone else tugging it. I'm called on this too: "Hey, you let go! No fair!" But I refuse to go into that closet.

"What are you afraid of?" asks Meredith in a needling sing-song. "Yeah, what are you afraid of?" the other girls echo, her teasing little puppets. They call me a baby. Am I a baby? At this moment, I don't care that I'm blowing all future sixth-grade social opportunities. All I want to do is crawl into my sleeping bag, head first.

I hate this Meredith. I am glad she lives on the other side of town and goes to Sutton. If she went to Francis Hopkinson, there would go the benign despotism of Mary Cat McAllister. I wonder if Mary Cat knows this would happen. I don't think she would care, so in thrall is she to this girl who keeps a pony in her backyard.

I get myself to sleep that night, hours after everyone else, by comforting myself with the thought that, after the morning, I will never see Meredith again.

•

Meredith once built a Barbie Dream House out of Barbie dolls — stacked hair to heels, the roof shingled with dismembered limbs and Barbie heads. It was a critique of domesticity, obviously, how the Barbie Dream House built expectations for a certain kind of life in a certain kind of body. She combed Goodwills and rummage sales for old dolls, asked her friends to contribute theirs. I donated mine, and she laughed when she saw them. As a child I had drawn on nipples and scribbled hair between their legs. I had been disturbed by their anatomical incorrectness.

The house gives me the creeps now. Those doll heads on the roof, staring at me, their blue eyes forever open beneath painted lashes. When I was dismantling the sculptures Meredith left behind, I went to yank off one of those heads and was knocked clear across the floor, as if I'd been shoved by a vengeful poltergeist. I haven't touched it since.

•

I told Meredith about Marie Bonaparte's theory about the distance between the clitoris and the vagina, and Meredith decided to make her own study, going Bonaparte one better by timing the measured subjects' minutes to orgasm. I told her it was a dumb idea, since Bonaparte was only interested in orgasms during intercourse, and if she were going to have them masturbate the clitoris might as well be in the crook of the arm — the distance from the vagina wouldn't enter into it. But Meredith said that was precisely the point; her project would engage in a dialogue between past assumptions about the female orgasm and what we know today. I thought the whole argument was moot — she'd never get enough volunteers.

We put up signs on campus with our address fanning out on a dozen tiny strips of paper. That Saturday, the line of women stretched down the block and around the corner twice. Tall women, short women, women in wheelchairs and women on crutches, black women, white women, the pierced and tattooed and the khakied and pearled. Our subjects were assigned a number, took off their panties and lay on the kitchen table. Meredith, wearing a white lab coat, held a metal ruler to each crotch and noted the measurement in millimeters on her clipboard. Then the subject would go into the bathroom with a stopwatch, and only a stopwatch — we had rules to level the playing field: fingers only, no Pocket Rockets or Hitachi Magic Wands — and emerge with a time, which I'd record on my clipboard. I wore a white lab coat too. Meredith's idea.

The bathroom was makeshift, three walls surrounding a toilet installed by Meredith, three walls that had a ways to go to meet the ceiling. The lack of privacy didn't seem to inhibit anyone, but listening to the moans of several hundred women for the eighteen hours we were in business was pretty surreal. I imagine it would be like working the popcorn concession in a porn theater. Do those places have popcorn?

Meredith didn't know what to do with the data. Maybe graph it, and then build a gigantic, three-dimensional representation of the graph out of wire hangers, those handy abortion-rights symbols that are almost as malleable as pipe cleaners.

Personally, I love pipe cleaners. Pipe cleaners and egg cartons and construction paper and rubber cement, the raw materials of preschool. We had a show at the museum of kids' work next to art made by professionals out of the same materials, and the kids' stuff was so much better. Sometimes I'd buy a pack of pipe cleaners just for the sensory flashback, watching the fuzz spring up as my fingers ran over it, bending and twisting the wire and then trying to bend it back the other way so it would look like untouched, virgin pipe cleaner. I was no artist — that was Meredith's job — so I didn't actually make anything out of the pipe cleaners. Just observed them. Observing — that was my job.

When you've decided to no longer participate in the world, just observe, it changes everything. You stop wanting, stop needing, because desire demands engagement with others. You merely watch, like an owl, or a lighthouse.

•

Meredith is dyslexic. That's what she says, anyway. Like many artists, she doesn't have the firmest grasp on the English language. "I'm a visual person!" she protests, exasperated by my constant theorizing. I have never been sure whether she truly believes in the superiority of vision over verbiage or if she just gets angry at her inability to catch my specious drift.

She truly is semiliterate, for which I hold her in contempt, dyslexia or no. There is no excuse, not with special ed and books on tape. She leaves notes for me in a child's chicken scrawl, her *n*s resolutely backward. Get "yogert + bred." She once wrote, "Please attack the screen door," so I yelled at it, tore it off its remaining hinge and stomped on it. She didn't think that was funny.

She hates my books. Take up too much room, she complains. I marvel at how she can write tortuous and tortured theoretical explanations of her work without having read any of the books she references. It is a certain skill she possesses, of which I am the slightest bit envious.

And I envy Meredith's perceptual gifts. Her intimacy with space and its possibilities. She could only be an artist. And I am an animal wrangler at a contemporary art museum, or I was, and I don't know what I am now.

•

We are lying next to each other on the battered yellow Salvation Army special, its upholstery reeking of grandmas and dust. Limbs intertwined, kissing the drowsy kisses of a marijuana-induced peace. A slip of a man, he fits on this couch flush against my body. I seem to prefer men who can get into my pants literally.

Meredith has gone to Stockholm to install a show. Michael showed up a couple of hours ago, looking for her. Gaunt, with the sucked-in cheeks of a British rock star, his speech already slurred to a crawl.

"You smoke?"

I invited him in, intending only the smoke. It had been a while, and he said it was the best, homegrown by a friend and tended by the sun.

He was right about the pot — it was the only time I've understood its appeal. There was no hydroponic headache, only the gentle haze the hippies must have known. This was the kind of pot you could smoke all day and never get sick, unlike that 200-proof crap byproduced by the War on Drugs.

As we make out on the couch, I think of my hippie uncle who once told me that back in his day, if you swung by your friend's pad and he wasn't there, his girlfriend would fuck you. No guilt or recriminations, just "love the one you're with." I am jealous of these people, so lucky to have come of age in that liberated era, and I am letting the strange hands of a strange man unzip my jeans because I want to live in that world.

Postcoitally, he tells me he's building a house up by the border where he's planning to raise goats and potatoes, he got his nose broken in a bar fight, he's got a kid by a common-law wife he met at an all-day Phish concert, and he wants to be some sort of youth counselor. He's created these non-confrontation cards to defuse teenage violence. One side has a situation like

"You're walking down the street and a stranger smacks you upside your head."

"Hey, that really happened to me."

"No way."

"Downtown, for real. This husky teenage girl, coming down the street with a whole pack of rowdy girls, just whacked me in the head for no reason. I thought someone should have come to my defense, but nobody did. It was a good whack, made a lot of noise. There's no way no one saw it."

"I'd have come to your defense."

"But aren't your cards supposed to de-escalate this sort of thing?"

"They're for teenagers who can't control their emotions. We're adults. Some teenage girl whacks you in the head, I have every right to take her down."

I run my hands over this 80-pound weakling, nudge his broken nose with my own and think, *Woe to the little man who thinks he can tangle with a broad-shouldered teenage girl.*

•

Michael is building his house entirely out of salvaged materials, and as a result it is a narrow rectangle, two floors of one hundred square feet each. The lower floor is entirely consumed by appliances — the wood-burning stove that heats the house, a small refrigerator, the sink and tub. All living is done upstairs, where the ceiling is low. The house does not yet have its fourth wall, so it resembles a stage set. This makes the sex, open to the valley below, kind of thrilling.

Afterwards I roll off his mattress onto the floor, taking in that barren land, wondering how he will grow anything with nine months of winter, but I say nothing.

"I'm not smart." He says this often, in a small voice, like he's stabbing himself in the chest with a tiny ice pick.

In his car, under the front passenger seat, I find a pack of *Non-confrontation Cards,* worn around the edges, copyright 1998. I shuffle them and cut the deck. The card reads, "You're walking down the street and a stranger smacks you upside your head."

I put the card in my pocket.

•

The sex has degenerated, as it always does, into a quick sawing and snoring. I have nothing to say to Michael. It has been well established that he has nothing to say to me. Still, he has driven down this morning, five hours, to pick me up and take me hiking in the mountains. As I throw my backpack in the backseat, he starts rolling a joint.

The pot has degenerated too — he crows that it's "premium skunkweed," inhaling its pungent oil from the bag, but it just makes my head pound. And there is no way, at 9 o'clock in the morning, that I am going to get in a car with a stoned driver. Not when I can't drive stick. There are certain risks, like sex with strangers, that really get me going. This is not one of them.

Okay. He ziplocks the bag and we're off. An hour later we stop for gas and the bag is out again. He yells at me, "You're not my mother!" I threaten to get out of the car and hitch back to the city.

"So get out of the car! See if I care!"

Then we're off again.

Five hundred feet up in the woods, we sit on the ground, our backs against a rock. I decline his offer to share. My head is pounding hard enough already.

Suddenly I've got his cock in my mouth — I don't know how it got there — and I am finding the greatest pleasure in expecting, and getting, nothing in return.

That evening, longing for confrontation, I flip the pack of non-confrontation cards at him, cascading them into his lap.

"Guess they weren't my idea, huh?"

I can't wring anything more from him. There is no confrontation.

I file the card under *M*.

•

I used to crave experience. But all experience is futile, I know that now. You think you're doing something new, but it's always the same. Heraclitus was wrong — you *can* step in the same river twice. You have to. There's only one river.

•

Marie Bonaparte had her clitoris moved three times. The first time she had it moved closer to her vagina; the second time to Vienna for several years of heavy-duty psychoanalysis with Sigmund Freud; the third time to the middle of the mantelpiece in Edgar Allan Poe's "The Purloined Letter," where Jacques Lacan would pretend not to find it.

This latter observation according to an essay by Barbara Johnson on a response by Jacques Derrida to a seminar by Jacques Lacan on "The Purloined Letter." You must have read it — Johnson's essay, that is — in Maximoff's Derrida and Deconstruction or Meltzer's Freud/Lacan/Psychoanalysis or Munshin's Intro to Poststructuralism. It is, in fact, the poststructural essay par excellence, an academic circle jerk of unparalleled emptiness.

All this for a short story about a stolen letter. But when Lacan, a purloiner of Saussurean linguistic theory, speaks of a "letter," he means both a piece of mail and a unit of the alphabet. So, since letters of the alphabet only have meaning in relation to other letters, we never learn the contents of the purloined letter, only that it takes on different meanings as it passes from one owner to another. The unconscious, Lacan might have said, is structured like a letter.

And this is no mere letter. Ever the lusty Frenchman, Lacan describes this errant bit of stationary as "an immense female body stretch[ed] out across the Minister's office," awaiting the ravishments of Poe's master detective, Monsieur Dupin. She's both vulnerable and intimidating — but not too intimidating, since her body can be penetrated, the puzzle solved.

Since Lacan is a good Freudian (or a bad one, depending on one's allegiance to Freud) he interprets the letter's purloining as the primal act of castration, at once the violence of birth and the nagging sensation the little girl has when she looks between her legs and wonders if something has been taken. The letter is thus the "lack," the wresting of the child from her mother, the urge to return to the womb that nourished us, to plug the hole; the origin of what we call "desire." The gaping fireplace above which the letter is found represents the vagina: the site of castration, the locus of lack.

Derrida points out that Lacan, an upstart who was fighting the French psychoanalytic establishment for the right to charge full fare for a five-minute session, has purloined this bit of analysis from Marie Bonaparte's psychobiography of Poe, without credit, except for one disparaging allusion to "the cook," since women belong in the kitchen, even the one who brought psychoanalysis to France. But there's a crucial difference between the cook and this Knave of Hearts: when Bonaparte calls the letter "phallic" she has in mind the actual organ, but for Lacan the phallus is, in his tortured language, "the privileged signifier of that mark where logos is joined together with the advent of desire." Derrida also punches holes in Lacan's analysis, accusing him of suffering an Oedipal conflict with the story's narrator (whom he omits entirely from his analysis in an attempt to build a classic psychoanalytic triangle) miscounting "scenes" in the story, and other crimes of "bad formalism."

Johnson, in her attempt to wrest the phallus from Derrida's slippery grasp, claims that if the central tenet of Derrida's deconstructionism is right — that you can never really know what anything means — then it is impossible to determine if Derrida's interpretation holds more or less water than Lacan's. This indeterminacy is rendered in bad puns: "Lacan's ills are really *ils*," "A 'Pli' for Understanding" (*pli* meaning "a rhetorical fold"). The poststructuralists find deep profundity in awful puns, which they consider "playful"; the translator of Lacan's "Seminar on 'The Purloined Letter'" is Jeffrey Mehlman — *Mailman, get it?* nudges Johnson. With the flourish of a master detective, Johnson reveals the letter *a* to be "the purloined letter par excellence in the writings of all three authors": Lacan's *objet a*, Derrida's *différance* and Poe's middle initial, taken from — aha! — his stepfather's surname. (And where is Poe in all this, you ask? Buried alive under the floorboards, his heart tick-tick-ticking while the poststructuralists read his last rites.)

If you think you're lost because you've never read "The Purloined Letter" — that rare Poe tale not to have been made into a Vincent Price movie, lacking as it does an Inquisitional torture chamber or a killer orangutan — know this: the story has itself been purloined: by Lacan to demonstrate the infallibility of his peculiar linguistics-inflected psychoanalysis, by Derrida to poke holes in that infallibility and thus work out his Oedipal baggage with Lacan, and by Johnson, who is too much the good little girl to want to kill either Father, as long as they'll let her play with their phallus. Being thus purloined, and (as Lacan asserts of the letter) its contents unknowable, you cannot actually read the story, since it is, in fact, missing.

But we are getting ahead of ourselves.

•

Camp Peaseblossom. Auditions are being held for the annual production of *A Midsummer Night's Dream*, to be performed by eleven-year-old girls in Mr. Manticore's much-abridged version. Since Shakespearean verse does not fall trippingly on the tongues of eleven year olds, the script has been modernized and unshackled from the demands of meter and rhyme. "Shall we their fond pageant see? Lord, what fools these mortals be!" has been rendered "Wanna go to the play? People are crazy!"

I stay up all night with a flashlight in my bunk, studying the real, undummied-down play. I am memorizing one of Puck's speeches. I cannot imagine auditioning to play Hermia or even Helena, even though she's kind of a dork — anyone who gets the guy, even if he's spellbound. And Titania will certainly be taken by one of the taller girls. Tall girls play queens, fat girls mothers. These are the rules of summer camp theatricals. So I am left with Puck, who must be small, being a faerie, and is kind of a gender-neutral meddler. I am comfortable with that.

The next morning I plant my bare feet on the grass and recite my monologue. "My mistress with a monster is in love!" My campmates applaud. And then Meredith gets up. She has not prepared a speech. She simply sits on the grass, does the most graceful of somersaults, and emerges upright with her legs crossed and arms outstretched like a Hindu idol. She gets the part. I end up playing Flute, the bellows-mender. That means that in the play-within-the-play the tradesmen put on, I play Thisby, the beloved of handsome Pyramus. Which is small compensation, playing a proto-Juliet played to hilarious incompetence by a man played to indulgent grins by an awkward girl.

I should hate Meredith, but instead I will write an essay about her when I return to school when that familiar question is posed: "Who is the most remarkable person you have ever met?" I will recall with admiration Meredith's effortless audition and repress my anger. I will not write about Backwards Day, when Meredith got everyone to put their bathing suits on backwards and when I chickened out they kicked me out of the cabin, singing "Go Away, Little Girl." I will also be wise enough to leave out a story revealed by flashlight, in a late-night game of Truth or Dare.

Meredith was walking down the street in her town, a town not too far from my own. Walking alone. And apparently her mother had never told her not to talk to strangers, because this funny old man came up to her, bought her an ice cream cone and took her to the back of a store. Cardboard boxes were piled high on steel shelves, and lights framed with black metal shutters loomed on towering stands like sunflowers, so bright you couldn't look at them. He asked her to take her clothes off, and she did. And then he took pictures of her. She insisted he was very nice.

And it was this confession that sparked the jealousy that has consumed me ever since. For I knew that, had I been walking down Meredith's street, that funny old man would never have picked me.

"But none of this is true," says Meredith. "I never went to Camp Peaseblossom. I've never been in a production of *A Midsummer Night's Dream*. I don't eat ice cream. I don't even know the words to 'Go Away, Little Girl.' We never met until the accident in the museum, at the carnival show."

She is mistaken. It was Camp Peaseblossom, the summer before seventh grade.

•

I've found a picture of Camp Peaseblossom. The group portrait you bring home to your parents at the end of the summer. Twenty-five girls in baby-blue Peaseblossom T-shirts. We're posed in three rows, two standing, one sitting. A prematurely developed girl stands in the back, a patch of sweat or spilled Hi-C crowning one proudly jutted-out breast. I'll bet she's embarrassed by that now. The short girls sit in front. I'm on the end with my legs crossed, my hair gathered in two fat, clumsy pigtails. They look like floppy dachshund ears.

Meredith is seated in the middle, holding one of those black signs with grooves for white peg letters. She is smiling that smile that melts camp drama coaches and misanthropic animal wranglers alike. I hate that smile, wish I could wipe it off her self-assured face. And she doesn't even remember that I was there.

•

"Marie Bonaparte had her clitoris moved three times," I tell Meredith.

"So you've told me," she says. I am boring her. This terrifies me. Boredom is always the beginning of the end.

·

It's a perfect Florida day, blue-skied and not too hot. Meredith and I have stopped off at one of those swim-with-a-dolphin joints in the Keys. She's been sent by a friend of a friend who works there, a perky blonde with light freckles and a seamless tan who trains the dolphins. She introduces us to the other women who work there, all perky blondes with light freckles and seamless tans. They look identical, like Stepford Wives. Dolphin geishas.

The intellectually disabled, she tells us, have much to gain from swimming with dolphins. It's been shown to be therapeutic for all kinds of disabilities. "Dyslexia?" I ask, and Meredith shoots me her dirtiest look.

This dolphin-swimming-as-therapy business disturbs me, the way horseback riding disturbed me as a child — some animal has been trained, has surrendered its freedom and autonomy, so that a human can feel better. How is this different from performing drug tests on animals? (I know, the dolphins don't die — but can they possibly be happy schlepping retards around the pool?)

I am in luck, and Meredith is out of hers. A dolphin attacked a customer this morning, and the whole pod is in lockdown while they figure out what went wrong. I'll tell you what went wrong — that dolphin, being smarter than your average sea cow, was tired of being some rich neurotic lady's stuffed toy. I am saved the ethical quandary of swimming with dolphins — because Meredith wants to do it, because I cannot turn down an experience swimming right in front of me. As consolation, our geisha takes us to meet one of the dolphins in training. As I kneel poolside and gingerly touch the short, wet hairs masking the slick skin underneath, I am suddenly seized by a fierce desire to wrap my arms around its neck and let it carry me out to sea.

Aelian recounts the tale of a dolphin who fell in love with a boy, with a tragic ending that must be quoted verbatim or you'll think I'm making it up:

> Thus, it happened that the boy exercised himself too vigorously, and in an exhausted state threw himself belly downwards on to his mount, and as the spike on the Dolphin's dorsal fin chanced to be erect it pierced the beautiful boy's navel. Whereupon certain veins were severed; there followed a gush of blood; and presently the boy died.

In his sorrow the dolphin, having fucked the boy to death, swam to shore and died on the beach beside his beloved.

I tell Meredith this story as we are driving away from the dolphins and their geishas, towards Key West and its T-shirt shops and condom baskets and Hemingway house full of cats.

"That's disgusting." Meredith has no patience with me today.

"It's kind of romantic, I think." It's not even Aelian's only tale of animal-boy love. "Admit it, at some point in your life, for one brief moment, you've thought about fucking an animal."

"Gross."

I had, once, in a rundown zoo, officially closed. I hadn't even known the zoo was there — I was just walking in the park, trying to get away from all those happy families pushing strollers, so I took a turn off the path and down into the brush to investigate some rooftops I had never noticed before. As I descended, the zoo emerged before me like a mirage. Graffiti obscured a riot of Beaux-Arts filigree, and I imagined couples strolling on a Sunday afternoon, the men in their top hats and monocles, the women in their bustles and parasols. A groundskeeper, old as the buildings, was tending to the last of the animals; nothing exotic, just the usual petting-zoo regulars — lambs, rabbits, a couple of decrepit cows.

He said the pandas, the alpacas and the giant rat had long been sold off. They were going to tear the whole thing down, put up a Wildlife Conservation Center.

"What's a Wildlife Conservation Center?"

"It's a place where you go to see animals."

"A zoo."

"Instead of bare cages, they'll be living in dioramas."

"Are they happier that way?"

"Who knows? But it makes the visitors happier."

A Potemkin village for animals. And now I saw the zookeeper in a Soviet uniform and Stalin moustache leading a detachment of dour schoolchildren in gray Mao jackets and bowl cuts through the warren of air-conditioned glass boxes destined to replace these ruins.

Alone in one of the pens was a scrawny, graying donkey, whose penis was so long it was dragging on the gravel. And for a moment, for I promised you there would be this moment, I wanted to lie down under it like I was Catherine the Great, and that donkey would bore so far into me that it would literally fuck my brains out.

•

Meredith and I are strolling through the new zoo —
pardon me, the wildlife conservation center. Like they're
kidding anybody. It's still an animal ghetto, an ark-load of
animals fenced inside an environment as bogus as a stage
set. No wonder the inmates lounge on the perimeter,
sluggish and unresponsive. A child tugs at his mother's
arm, crying, "Mommy, I think he's dead!" No, kid, he's
just waiting for feeding time. He's got nothing to do but
idle near the wings, as off-stage as he can get, as if he
could escape to a freedom just beyond his confines.

•

Some nights I find myself haunted by a painting, a large
canvas by Melchior d'Hondecoeter commissioned for a
Utrecht merchant's well-appointed dining room. Against
a backdrop of artfully distressed ruins, two peacocks
are perched on a block of stone, one with its feathers
in glorious cascade, the other poised to prey on a spider
monkey. The monkey is eyeing an oversized, overfed
squirrel, which is eyeing him back while pawing an acorn
as big as its head. There are the expected still-life clichés
of glassy grapes, peaches and a luscious split melon, but
could this monkey, too, be destined for dinner? A small
turkey stares, a red-necked crane gazes the customary
left, and, wholly uninvolved, a black bird with a dash of
red on its forehead flies through the sky, painted as if by
afterthought. The latter is the only animal that does not
seem truly alive, a decorative dollop of whipped cream on
a tableau engineered for maximum appetite stimulation.

This fantastic, too-peaceable kingdom seems on
the verge of erupting into violence. The peacock will

swoop down on the monkey, who will be caught in the proverbial middle as it lunges for the squirrel.

Meredith is creating her own Peaceable Kingdom with stuffed animals. She's dedicating it to me, chattering on about animals as I do. "Maybe it'll shut you up," she says.

She's got piles of toy animals on the floor. Old teddy bears with pilling polyester fur. A well-loved lion with a mane of twisted brown yarn, a fiberglass rocking horse, a barnyard menagerie of plastic cows and sheep, wooden dogs with wheels for paws. A child's garden of elephants, giraffes, fang-toothed walruses, in unholy shades of orange, pink and fluorescent purple. A Mickey Mouse and a Bugs Bunny. A half-dozen Beatrix Potter anthropomorphs, almost as small as the books they once accompanied. Even a couple of the more animal-resembling Pokémon.

"I don't think those really belong."

"You always take things so literally. The lion lies down with the lamb, Peter Rabbit lies down with the Pokémon. Children don't discriminate between the verisimilitudinous animal and the mouse in short pants. But cartoon characters come and go; the teddy bear persists."

Verisimilitudinous? I'm impressed. I am beginning to rub off on her. "Do you love me?" I want to ask, trembling, but it can't find its way out of my throat. Instead I grab the stuffed lion and roll on my back, pressing my nose into his, wiggling and giggling.

"Hey, I need that," barks Meredith. I toss the lion at her. Damn creative types, so fucking focused on their work. When she gets like this — when I get like this, all mushy and emotional — one of us has to get some air, and it is always me.

It is, after all, her storefront. I just live here.

•

You were expecting a plot?

"You have to give them a plot," says Meredith. "No one will read this far without one. They've done studies."

Have they? It seems to me that if "The Purloined Letter" has no plot (save the plot to steal the letter) then I shouldn't need one either. It also seems to me that the architecture of plot, at least as delineated by Aristotle as rising action building to a climax and falling swiftly into resolution, derives from male sexual response — we *are* talking about the Greeks, all that man-boy, dolphin-boy love — and to adopt that form is to suffer the self-mutilation of Marie Bonaparte, to give up one's female experience for a facsimile of a man's. I'm not saying that women cannot tell good stories; but in doing so we deny an essential part of our own experience, a sexuality that is nonlinear, irregular, unpredictable.

Meredith always laughs when I go off on this subject. "You think you're going to change the habits of readers who have had their expectations molded by centuries of patriarchy, that they will slog through a book that's going nowhere just because it's the right thing to do. No, they will get bored. No one — no woman — will indulge you. You'd better give people something to read."

"I'm a little stuck right now."

"I *thought* you were rationalizing your way out of writer's block."

"That's not fair! How come you can get away with all your feminist theories and I can't get away with mine?"

"It's different. The art world is less judgmental; everyone pretends to be so critical, but no one wants to be the one who doesn't get it. And let's face it, art is less demanding of people's time. You walk through a gallery, stand in front of a pile of stuffed animals, sipping your wine. Reading a book is a commitment — all those pages, all those hours — that's why I never finish them. You want people to read your book, you've got to give them a plot."

"Like you said, I'm a little blocked."

"Tell them how we met. Change a few insignificant details. You know what to do."

•

And so I begin. Three years ago, sitting in the back of Mankiewicz's Dutch Realist Paintings of the Seventeenth Century. Today, the curious subgenre of dead bird paintings. The slides blur before my tired eyes. Van Beyeren. Van Aelst. Van der Meer.

Cornelis Lelienbergh codified the plain perfection of the dead bird still life in his studio in The Hague. His paintings are comfortingly formulaic, subtle variations on a theme. Always a large dead bird, one leg nailed to a drab wall. Always an arrangement of smaller birds on a table below. His palette eschews nameable color, save the light on the hanging bird illuminating its uncooperatively blooming plumage.

The conventions of the Lelienbergh still life will be tremendously influential on his colleagues. Abraham Bloemaert and Elias Vonck will keep that spotlight trained on the hanging bird. Melchior d'Hondecoeter will paint that dull wall *trompe l'oeil*. Barend van der Meer will keep the wall pale but drench the hanging bird in saturated colors imported from Italy by Jan Baptist Weenix and Willem van Aelst. Van Aelst will turn the whole subgenre on its head by painting his hanging birds in the cold light of day, rather than the Dutch eternal twilight, paradoxically rendering the plumage of the dead vibrantly alive.

Why dead birds? How do you think artists survived the Protestant Reformation? What does one paint when one can no longer paint Jesus? All that is left is capitalism, and if you lacked the talent for capturing the prosperous pink faces of commissioning merchants, you specialized. In landscapes, or still life. Flowers, fruit, the breakfast piece (early and late), banquets (lobster, oysters, wine, fruit, lemon half-peeled into a spiral á la Willem Kalf — now he knew how to paint a lemon peel!), pronk (golden goblets, Oriental ceramics, Venetian glass), vanitas (skulls on top of books, shells, candles, ivy, perhaps a lute), the spoils of the hunt, dead fish. You paint those pasty scales over and over, you start to get really good at it. It's fair to say that seventeenth century Holland produced not only the most paintings of dead animals, but also the best.

A later evolution of the dead birds still life, after the birds-nailed-to-a-wall, is the "Falconer's Bag." We are looking at a typical example by Jan Weenix, son of Jan Baptist, nephew of d'Hondecoeter. In a Venetian paradise only a Dutchman could imagine, in which canals provide passage for both gondoliers and swans (how did *they* escape the falconer's aim?), a pile of dead birds is displayed before us. The prize bag, a great heron, gazes with a glazed-over eye at the lobster-claw bird whistle in the bottom left corner, its beak on the same diagonal as the mouth of the hunter's horn under its feathers and the customary stone pillar above. In the foreground two small birds lie, one ruddy-feathered, the other dove-white, one's head resting on the other's belly. Their beaks face each other, as if they might kiss. Are they lovebirds? I wonder, is there really such a species as lovebird?

Behind the heron rest at least three dead birds. There is no blood, no evidence of violence, of the taking of these lives. A duck's beak juts out from above the hunting horn. A rack of feathers, wrested from another bird, is nearby, disembodied and disused. In front of it all is slung the falconer's leather belt, brass-buckled with attached scissors, and blooming below the pillar the great heron's analogue, a large pink flower among orange and tiny red blossoms. But the blossoms look fake, too brilliant, borrowed from another painting. These flowers disturb me — the subdued Dutch palette of this period soothes my latent Puritanism, Rembrandt browns so much warmer than those unseemly Frans Hal pinks. Weenix — the name sounds like what you'd call the shrimpiest kid on the playground — has inscribed his name on top of the pillar, which seems immodestly un-Dutch, as if to say, "These are my spoils. *I* am the falconer."

Marcel is passing notes to me, as usual. But this one isn't a note; it's a $10,000 check to go to bed with him. I pocket the check, stifling a giggle.

We are looking at another Weenix. This one's huge, overwhelming and decadent, as the homestretch of a genre's inning always are. In another quasi-Italian landscape of strolling courtiers, a white swan, that most prized bag, and a peacock lie dead at the foot of marble stairs. Smaller birds litter the foreground. The swan's beak and wings tilt upward, the final erection of the dead. A stone cherub peers down over them, holding an empty, outpoured urn. Ivy twists around the cherub's body; below his feet a gargoyle scowls. A collie bays at the dusk, his head tilted straight to the sky like the swan's beak, no longer at the service of nature, or man, but of eye-pleasing geometry. The dog's upturned snout leads the eye to a statue of a hawk on a pedestal, eternally alive, eternally dead. A couple of birds fly away, free for the time being.

Another check. $20,000, this time made out to me and someone named Meredith. "Do you know her?" he murmurs in his childlike drawl, luxuriating in each vowel like the Frenchman he is. He is pointing to a light-brown shag several rows down. "If we all have sex together, you can split the check."

I laugh. I know he hasn't got a dime.

•

Marcel and I have a curious relationship: platonic, on account of a nasty and recurring sexually transmitted disease he says he has. Or maybe I'm just not his type.

Since fall we have been inseparable, every meal, every movie at the Film Society. *Alphaville. The Conformist. Children of Paradise.* Marcel makes films — make that one film he is constantly re-editing — in which his enormous, Frankenstein-rectangle of a head, shot from a 16mm Bolex held at arm's length, jerks around against a psychedelic backdrop. At 19 he already has one patron, a performance artist who projects his films as backdrops for spectacles staged in parking lots in which giant robots rip each other to pieces and explode.

At first I laugh off the checks, but as the weeks pass Marcel seems to have forgotten his allegedly oozing sores. I keep laughing, so Marcel starts hanging around with this Meredith. I begin to see less of him, and more of them in a corner in the Commons, eating silently. At the Film Society, with her. *The World of Apu. Pickpocket. Red Desert.*

He is still all mine in the back of art history class.

"You sure you don't know her?" he asks of the back of that light-brown head. "I think you do."

Today we have moved on to the equally curious subgenre of dead fish paintings. Abraham van Beyeren is the undisputed master of the dead fish, although he was underappreciated in his day, as all geniuses are. Pieter de Putter, Harmen Steenwyck, Jan Vonck — they tried, but perhaps only Isaac van Duynen could paint an assortment of fish on a wooden table almost as well as van Beyeren.

Like Cornelis Lelienbergh's birds, van Beyeren's fish are inserted into a rigorous structure. Always a few in the foreground, a pile in a wicker basket behind them. In his larger paintings there's often a second basket of fish under the table. The fish, knives, kettles and vegetables are arranged on diagonals originating at the bottom corners of the paintings. Sometimes he adds a window in the background, opened to the coast and distant fishermen. Ever the tasteful Dutchman, van Beyeren's colors are muted, save the burning red of a salmon steak or the belly of a trout, glistening like silver.

This slide, a typical Van Beyeren, shows three or four fish on the table, the frontmost one hacked into thick accordion slices. Its eyes stare off to the left, as did Weenix's falcon, as do the lobsters in Dutch banquet paintings, always, always, and I wonder what's lurking there, just beyond the edge of the canvas. There's a rope tied around one fish, and in the basket another upside-down, its mirror image, sliced straight down its middle but not to the skin, its eye turned back, dead and away. Behind it a fish steak glows orange-red, seemingly not of animal born. A ladle rests against its pot; a bouquet of white radishes awaits. Among the muted browns, the only deep color radiates from the severed flesh.

I try to pass Marcel a note, but he looks lost in inscrutable thought.

"What's up with you and Marcel?" people ask. In the Commons. At the Film Society. *Rashomon. La Dolce Vita. Jules and Jim.*

I find myself a new Film Society companion, Mickey Fish. (I'm not making this one up; that's really his name.) Mickey suffers from a sort of G-rated Tourette's. Throughout the movie he will blurt out meaningless monosyllables — "Yuh," "Um," "Wuh." He tries to casually drop his hand on my thigh. *Hiroshima Mon Amour. Shoot the Piano Player. Bonnie and Clyde.*

My attention drifts to Marcel. He sits with Meredith in class now and I scrutinize each tip of their heads and shrug of their shoulders for meaning. *Belle du Jour. The Bicycle Thief. Johnny Guitar.*

And then, one day, without explanation, Marcel is again in the back of the lecture hall, passing me notes. But now instead of checks I get pornographic doodles in which one figure is supposed to be me, the other that light-brown head a few rows in front. I roll my eyes. "It's true," he whispers.

The whole thing comes to a head (ah, that damn climax, can't get away from it) at the end-of-semester art show, for which Marcel has submitted a collage of advertisements for liquor and cigarettes from old magazines, hard and decoupaged, forming a frame around its centerpiece, a pictorial from a '70s porn magazine about two lifelessly pretty women with long straight hair, unenlarged breasts and floppy straw hats sunning themselves on a topless beach on the French Riviera. As I walk into the gallery I feel all eyes upon me, waiting for me to read the copy, about how these best friends love to vacation together, they said, as one idly rubbed suntan lotion on her friend's nipple.

"Idly" — I remember that word. By the last page one of the girls had pulled down the other's bottom, her tongue aimed serpent-like towards her friend's finely haired crotch, but not touching, in the convention of soft-core pornography. A still life, I think.

Arrows have been drawn in Magic Marker, the girls labeled. The one with the outstretched tongue is me. Scrawled over the whole spread are more words, the handwriting familiar. Meredith and I are sitting in a tree, k-i-s-s-i-n-g.

This sends me crying to the Dean of Students, who suspends Marcel for a week. That's where I met Meredith, in the Dean's office. Only she wasn't crying. She just sat there, legs crossed, calmly flipping through the alumni magazine.

"But that's not how we met at all," says Meredith, reading these last few pages. "I never took any class on Dutch Realist painting — how boring! The two-semester Art History requirement was enough for me, all those slides of Michelangelo crap, Leonardo crap…."

Sometimes I just want to smack her.

"Tell them how we met for real," she continues. "At Camp Peaseblossom. Mr. Manticore's production of *A Midsummer Night's Dream.*"

•

I once read that mankind evolved as a tool-making creature because it could not compete as a carnivore with the great cats and dogs of the jungle, whose senses were more highly evolved. Domesticating cats and dogs is, I think, man's revenge.

It may come as a surprise to you that Meredith had a cat prowling around, since there were birds flying all over the place, or as no surprise, if you're going by the stereotype of two women living together. It will also come as no surprise that I hated that haughty, good-for-nothing creature, licking herself, lurking under the sofa, scratching in the litter box. She didn't care much for me either.

We are taking Malinka to the vet to be spayed. (Even the names of pets have been changed to protect their privacy.) Until this day I didn't really know what spaying entailed. It's an ovariohysterectomy, says Meredith. I gasp. It's good for her, she says. Humane, even.

It will keep her from littering the world with unwanted kittens. It will put an end to the nuisances of heat — howling, peeing on the carpet. It will prevent uterine infections, cancer even. "Why don't we get spayed too?" I ask. "Won't be distracted by that pesky sex drive anymore. Or worry about cancer. In fact, let's get everything removed that could possibly get cancer. Breasts, lymph nodes, spleen…."

Meredith doesn't find this funny. But I wonder about Malinka, waking up after the isoflurane has worn off, no longer suffering the desire that makes life worth living. She will be rendered merely decorative, a living toy. And this, Meredith says, is humane. It's for her own good.

They once told women it was for their own good. In 1936 in *Diseases of Infancy and Childhood,* the primary pediatric text of its era, L. Emmett Holt prescribed clitoral cauterization for frequent masturbators. And in some parts of Africa, still today. Marie Bonaparte first learned of such customs from London anthropology student and future Kenyan Prime Minister Jomo Kenyatta, who assured her that girls were quite willing, eagerly awaiting their initiation into womanhood. Marie was suitably horrified, and reported these rites to Dr.

Freud who, in disbelief that any culture would modify the body in a way that wouldn't be pleasurable for both parties, assured her that women must get something out of it. As Marie would discover when she visited Africa, they did — the old women wielding the sharpened flint, searing the teenage clitoris with a rock heated to the temperature of an iron, taking her vengeance on the next generation.

•

In "Of custom, and not easily changing an accepted law" Montaigne lists female circumcision as part of a "Believe It or Not" two pages long, beginning: "There are countries where, except for the wife and children, no one speaks to the king except through a tube...." The list goes on to itemize such foreign curiosities as nose-piercing and the ability to swim and use a bow and arrow at the same time.

•

Dr. Freud gave Marie a book, *Neger-Eros* by the Swedish anthropologist Felix Bryk, which reports the traditions of the Nandis, who live on the slopes of Mt. Elgon in East Africa and burn off their daughters' clitorises at eighteen. Bryk writes that the ritual helps along the process of sexual maturation by moving the site of orgasm from the clitoris to the vagina; the Nandis are thus Freudians *avant la lettre*. If a woman does not submit, any subsequent babies she has will have the life throttled out of them.

I get this secondhand, from Bonaparte's *De la sexualité de la femme* (1951). The public library has never heard of *Neger-Eros,* or Bryk, or the Nandis, for that matter.

•

But Marie must see this firsthand. On her way to see Professor Mahfouz Pasha, a gynecologist at the Coptic Hospital in Cairo, she feels a discomfort she has never known on the boulevards of Paris. Men hiss at her in the street, as they do all shameless European women, hurling their basest epithet, "Mother of the clitoris." But they insult her in Arabic, which she does not understand.

Dr. Pasha explains that excision routinely takes place before the age of ten, as it has for centuries. Unwrap a mummy and you won't find a clitoris. Cleopatra, excised. The most famous female sex symbol of all time, clitless.

He takes her to a patient: "The excised labia minora were welded together over the stump of the clitoris," she will write. "Touch it," he urges, as if it were not still part of another woman's body. Marie demurs. "You are a scientist," he says. "Touch it." And she does, stifling unscientific tears.

She asks Dr. Pasha if she can interview his patients, ask them about their sexual response, their marital bliss or lack thereof. But he denies her request, as it can only lead to scandal.

•

In an unspoken African country, Marie visits Mrs. A, a forty-year-old mother of three, excised at six by the village witch. She explains that the purpose of the operation is to "diminish female sensuality in hot climates." Although she claims she has "fully vaginal" orgasms, she refuses to have her daughters' clitorises excised, due to the extreme pain she experienced during and after the operation.

In another unnamed African country, Marie meets Mrs. B, thirty years old, excised at 11. Her father deceased, her mother insisted on the operation, over the protests of her uncles. Here alcohol is dabbed on the clitoris to inhibit its development. Since the clitoris stayed small, the old woman burned off more than was required. After the operation she hemorrhaged and the wound was infected. She estimates that one out of every three times she has sex she reaches orgasm, a success rate Bonaparte credits to Mrs. B's enjoyment of penetration, unlike Marie, whose displeasure in intercourse is so strong that she must use "unconscious sword-swallower's psychology" to get through the act.

After Marie has left, Mrs. B's husband tickles her scar to orgasm.

•

In Mali, they excise girls at 12. The ritual is performed by an old woman of the blacksmith caste. No painkillers are used. After butter and herbs have been slathered on the place where their clitoris and inner labia were only minutes before, the initiates are commanded to dance, blood and butter running down their legs.

On our tour of "the land of the sewn women," as our guide calls Somalia, a little girl, two little hands on a little cane, inches herself towards us. As she gets closer we see the string dangling between her legs, holding a nest of thorns piercing the wound where her inner labia once were. Like the thorns that climb the walls of Sleeping Beauty's tower, they are intended to keep the most ardent suitors away. Balancing the high price of virginity with the biological imperative to excrete, a matchstick juts out from between her legs. It will be pulled out when she has to go to the bathroom, and replaced as soon as she has finished, until a urethral hole has made itself a place in the wound.

One of her younger friends lies on the ground, her legs bound like her vaginal lips. She will remain like this for a month, perhaps more.

Another has been betrothed, and in preparation for marriage the old woman has cut some of the stitches and inserted a wooden dildo to stretch her out. I was surprised to see this — I had thought that one of the purposes of infibulation was to ensure a tight, virginal hole, but apparently all they care about is the virginal part. In Somalia, anyway. Because now we are in the Sudan on a wedding night, as the husband takes a knife to the threads. And now we are in Southern Egypt. This bride's vagina has all but disappeared. The groom pushes his way in through the mass of scar tissue between her legs. He has opiated himself just enough to maintain an erection while enduring her screams.

This one has miscarried, the fetus unable to evacuate the mother's sewn vagina; the dead body will kill the live one. This one is giving birth, arms above her head, strung up like a pig to be disemboweled. This one has just had a baby, and is being sewn up all over again. The old woman now leaves room for the husband's penis, and will cut the rest of the threads to permit childbirth. The procedure will be repeated after each pregnancy.

This one has reached old age. Her husband died of malaria when she was thirty, at which point the old woman sewed her up for good. And now she is that old woman, taking the little girls to the hut, cutting off their inner labia and stitching them up with thread. Sewing has always been women's work.

In the West, it is a man's.

Marie Bonaparte writes of a Leipzig woman, one Frau R., who masturbated compulsively, as often as fifteen times a day, but was otherwise unsatisfied. In her mid-thirties, from 1928 to 1929, she underwent three operations. Her clitoris and inner labia, ovaries and fallopian tubes were removed; all nerves were severed. She still failed to orgasm with her husband. Her psychiatrist, Dr. Herbert Weigel, reported that "The husband seems to be clumsy in their relations, and carries out coitus without preliminaries." Frau R. showed Marie where she continued to touch herself — exactly where the clitoris had been.

Bonaparte ascribes this curiosity to "the dominance of the 'dynamic stereotyping' of the autonomous nervous system (this woman went on feeling her clitoris as cripples do their amputated leg or arm…)." At night Marie continues to touch her own scar; she cannot help herself.

The Victorians believed that circumcising the clitoral hood would control masturbatory hysteria by reducing sensitivity, much as removing the foreskin did in boys. And if that didn't work, they removed the temptation itself. In his 1866 *On the Curability of Certain Forms of Insanity, Epilepsy, Catalepsy, and Hysteria in Females,* Isaac Baker Brown detailed his achievements in clitorectomy, and was promptly kicked out of the London Obstetrical Society. American doctors read Brown's book, and within a couple of decades Dr. E.H. Pratt had founded Chicago's Orificial Surgery Society, which held that atypical clitoral hoods were the problem. If the hood hugged the clitoris like a laced-to-death corset, an incision would be made to give it room to breathe.

A tight clitoral hood was soon blamed for a host of problems. In a 1915 article in the *American Journal of Clinical Medicine,* Dr. Benjamin E. Dawson of Kansas City wrote that it could lead to "convulsions, eczema, paralysis, constipation, tuberculosis, locomotor ataxia, rheumatism, idiocy, insanity, lust and all its consequences." To his credit, Dr. Dawson did not think children should be punished for masturbating. They couldn't help it if their tight prepuce was stimulating them inordinately.

Dr. Dawson cites his success with a two-and-a-half year old who was wasting away and did not yet speak. "The clitoris was completely snowed under," he writes, and while the child was under general anesthesia he took hold of the clitoral hood with Pratt's plug forceps, yanked it up, and cut a narrow triangle out of its center. He then stitched the apex with catgut and sent the little girl home with orders to pull the remaining hood back daily. When the mother failed to follow through, the girl was back in his office, the hood adhering to her clitoris again, and he performed the operation once more. Her clitoris freed, the girl gained weight, took long-overdue baby steps and made long-overdue baby talk.

He recounts the case of a weeks-old baby with colic, cured by circumcision. A two-year-old with kidney trouble and an incorrigible attitude transformed into a healthy child of easy disposition. A seven-year-old who couldn't stop touching herself. A sixteen-year-old bedwetter. A 46-year-old nymphomaniac. Older patients were spared the risks of general anesthesia — a swabbing of ten-percent cocaine solution followed by an injection of four-percent cocaine into the hood did just fine.

Not that the good doctor saw deformity wherever he looked. "Only two days ago a physician brought a lady to me for circumcision," he writes. "Everything ready, I started to do the work, when a normal clitoris smilingly said, 'Keep off the grass, please.'"

As we move into the supposedly repressed '50s these operations continued. Circa 1959, Dr. W. G. Rathmann of Centinela Hospital in Inglewood, California was recommending circumcision in cases of anatomically based frigidity. He also advised that the surgery be done if the patient was obese, if her clitoris was too small, or if her husband couldn't find it.

Of particular concern to Dr. Rathmann was not just the adhesive hood but the "redundant" hood, classifying both on a 1–4 scale. He pried it back with pliers of his own invention, to be used exclusively on female genitalia. Photographed with jaws opened and closed, they look like a metal duck with a screw for an eye, quacking its wide duckbill. He smeared a wax of benzocaine and terramycin on the area to prevent readhesion, sent the patient home with a bottle of Percodan, and saw her every couple of days for the next two weeks to make sure the wax had done its job. Women who had the surgery on Friday could be back to work on Monday.

In 1973 New York gynecologist Leo Wollman was still cutting off the clitoral hoods of Park Avenue's Most Frigid. In response to a 1977 California lawsuit detailing the distress of a patient who was unhappy with the outcome of the operation, the chairman of the OB-GYN Department at Stanford testified that such operations were "a matter of judgment."

And today doctors offer something called "designer vaginoplasty." Some have traded in their scalpels for lasers. They have offices on Fifth Avenue and Rodeo Drive; in France it's a covered medical expense. They will trim your inner labia, sculpt them, liposuck fat out of the tops of your thighs and inject it into your outer labia to plump them up, suture your vaginal wall muscles, tighten your pubococcygeus and transverse perineal muscles to make accessible that elusive G-spot, even repair your hymen, erasing years of intercourse and childbirth. Like a virgin, but more "aesthetically pleasing," as the ads say. And multiorgasmic, they promise, all in one hour under local anesthesia.

•

"This is all very interesting, but I think you've lost the plot." Meredith tends to get fidgety when a few pages go by without her.

"It's not all about you," I say.

"We were taking Malinka to the vet…"

"But nothing happened at the vet."

"Well, something's got to happen somewhere. You keep going on about Marie Bonaparte's clitoris. What happened to that?"

And so I continue.

•

Marie Bonaparte's clitoris was moved three times. After her death, that is. The initial removal has been obscured by gossip — some say it was severed by an intrepid mortician, or that her grave was robbed. The most pernicious rumor is that Dr. Halban failed to reattach it during Marie's third operation — it just couldn't take any more stitches, the poor thing. It is said that he gave it to her in a glass jar, mounted on a pin like a butterfly. And that she left it to her friend Ruth, now Mack-Brunswick, who had been at her side for every operation. Or that Mack-Brunswick stole it from Dr. Halban, who was saving it as a specimen alongside the African and Arab clitori that Marie had brought him from the operations she observed, and Marie was none the wiser.

It is said that as the years went on, Mack-Brunswick's morphine addiction grew such that she was compelled to sell the clitoris to one of her medical colleagues for a fix. That it came into the possession of Anna Freud as she was combing through her father's archives at Berggasse 19. That it was supposed to be included in the Smithsonian's controversial Sigmund Freud exhibit that toured this great nation some time ago, alongside bundled rough drafts and the Ur-couch — but that Ripley's moment never happened, because when the keepers of the Freud archives went looking for the clitoris, it could not be found.

All of which has turned Marie Bonaparte's clitoris into the holy grail of Freudian psychoanalysis, clinging as it is for shreds of meaning in an HMO'd world. There are men who have spent their careers searching for it, the sort of men who enroll in psychoanalytic training institutes these days — not doctors, but Sanskrit scholars who have lost their way and burnt-out roadies who never found it. They do not practice, these psychoanalysts, patients being superfluous in their heady, theoretical world.

There are no women searching for Marie Bonaparte's clitoris.

•

Okay, I'll fess up — Marie Bonaparte's clitoris is here, mounted on a pin in a jar by the door. Who is it for? All the lonely people.

I can't tell you how it got here. I'm not sure I know myself. It might be Meredith's. She's always picking up odd junk for sculptures.

I don't even know if it's really her clitoris. It's *somebody's* clitoris. It says it's Marie's; might as well take it at its word.

The clitoris and I got acquainted one night while I was pondering the finer incisions of Barbara Johnson's paper on Jacques Derrida's paper on Jacques Lacan's paper on "The Purloined Letter," the gist of which I believe I've already gisted, although when I'm finished writing I intend to throw up all these pages into the air and let them fall where they may. I had decided that I should actually read "The Purloined Letter" to see what the fuss was about. Finding that "The Purloined Letter" was not in fact missing at all (it was right here in *The Portable Poe*), I read the opening epigraph by Seneca, shuddered, and returned the book to its pile.

"You're wasting your time on nonsense," said the clitoris.

"Tell me about it."

"A paper about a paper about a paper about a really dumb story in which nothing happens, just blab, blab, blab. I could understand all this effort going into 'The Fall of the House of Usher,' but 'The Purloined Letter'? This policeman visits Monsieur Dupin, tells him he's looking for a letter stolen from some royal lady's *boudoir* by one Minister D—— — and why do they have the same last initial, huh? — and recounts how they turned the thief's place upside down. He returns a month later, and — *voilà!* — Dupin produces the letter and explains how he found it. The End. No action. Just characters relating what they did, interrupted by digressions about odds and evens and why $x^2 + px$ does not always equal q. That's not a story."

"Academics like the digression about the marbles. And the erudite allusions to the Greeks."

"Ah, nothing is more hateful to wisdom than cleverness," sighed the clitoris. "You want to hear a real story?"

"Why not?" I shrugged.

And the clitoris began:

"Once upon a time, on the muddy banks of the lower delta of the Daisymactawphaw River, lived Maisy Bumble and her twin sisters Trisky and Crumble Dee. Many years ago their parents were killed by a mountain lion right before their very eyes, and Maisy had taken care of her sisters ever since. But now that her charges were old enough to look after themselves, Maisy Bumble had decided it was time to go out and seek her fortune.

"'I am going to seek my fortune,' said Maisy Bumble.

"She wrapped in a kerchief some rolls, a couple of hard-boiled eggs, an apple, and a handful of Band-Aids, tied the kerchief to a stick, stuck a slingshot in her back pocket, kissed her teary sisters goodbye and headed out into the world.

"Maisy walked for days and nights, past fields and marshes, puddles and streams, past forests and oil rigs and whirling wind-powered generators. She walked until her legs ached and her eyes burned and her head spun, and when that happened she curled up by the side of the road and went to sleep. She got leaves in her hair and dirt under her nails and bugs between her teeth. She ate the rolls, the hard-boiled eggs and the apple, and then fruit from the trees and berries from the bushes. Sometimes she ate the wrong berries and got sick, but since she had suffered this back on the muddy banks of the lower delta of the Daisymactawphaw River, she knew what to expect.

"After many weeks of wandering, with nary a soul to guide her way, Maisy Bumble began to despair of ever finding her fortune.

"'Oh, I will never find my fortune!' she cried.

"Just then a mountain lion emerged from the bushes. He looked just like the mountain lion who had killed Maisy's parents those many years ago! But then, all mountain lions looked alike to Maisy Bumble.

"'Halt!' cried Maisy Bumble. 'Are you the mountain lion that killed my parents?'"

"A little formal, don't you think?" I muttered.

The clitoris frowned. "How about this then: The mountain lion bounded towards Maisy, drool trickling from the corner of his mouth, claws poised for dissection."

"Better."

"Although nearly paralyzed by exhaustion, Maisy suddenly darted, quick as a jackal. She grabbed a stone, pulled her slingshot out of her back pocket, and struck the mountain lion right between the eyes, knocking him flat.

"'That was really uncalled for,' moaned the mountain lion."

"Oh, it's one of those talking animal stories," I groaned.

"It's a fable," snapped the clitoris.

"Then *all* the characters have to be animals."

"Well, it's got a moral. And I'll never get to it if you keep interrupting me."

I leaned back on the carpet, my feet resting on top of a set of 1978 Compton's Encyclopedias, raw material for one or another of Meredith's projects, and let the clitoris continue.

"The mountain lion wept. 'I wasn't attacking you,'

he said. 'No one ever comes out this way, and I've been so lonely. I was just happy to see you.'

"Maisy dropped her slingshot and crept towards the weeping mountain lion, cradling his head in her arms. She stroked his fur and wept a little herself. 'A mountain lion killed my parents,' she whispered.

"'Some of my brothers can be so cruel,' sobbed the mountain lion.

"'It was a long time ago.' They remained in an embrace until the wind grew stronger and the sun grew dim.

"'Where are you bound?' asked the mountain lion.

"'I am off to seek my fortune,' said Maisy Bumble.

"'Which means what, exactly?'

"'I don't know, really. I've been walking for what seems like forever, and now I've run out of food, and my legs ache and my eyes are burning and my head is pounding and I don't know where my fortune lies.'

"'Come with me, then,' said the mountain lion. 'I am returning to claim my throne in my kingdom on the Yakteree. I've been in exile these many years, wandering, just like you. But those who deposed me have been defeated, and I would be most honored if you would join me as my queen.'

"Maisy thought for a moment. 'This is where I kiss you and you turn into a handsome prince, right?'

"'No, I'm really a mountain lion. What do you say?'

"Could Maisy Bumble love a mountain lion? She gazed into his soulful eyes and stroked his sumptuous fur coat, longing to sink deep into it, to wrap it around her dwindling frame. And so the two wanderers set out to reclaim the mountain lion's kingdom on the Yakteree.

"The journey to the mountain lion's kingdom was long and treacherous, but Maisy and the mountain lion found great pleasure in each other's company, singing, 'Valderee, Valderah!' as they marched along. Maisy found advantages to traveling with the mountain lion, for his roar kept predators away and his teeth and claws proved more effective than her slingshot in trapping dinner. He taught her to eat her meat raw. She taught him to retract his claws when he caressed her. At night, when they curled up under the glowing moon, Maisy's tanned limbs enveloped by the warmth of the mountain lion's fur, they were at once truly together and alone in the world.

"At length they reached a lake, and Maisy stripped off her tattered jeans and dove in. The mountain lion, being none too fond of water, waited for her on the bank, admiring her smooth skin and graceful strokes. But Maisy had another admirer lurking in the woods — the mountain lion that killed her parents! His dispatch of the once and future king of the Yakteree was swift and brutal, and he dragged the corpse into the woods before Maisy, who had swum out too far to hear her friend's cries, emerged from the lake. So when Maisy Bumble and the mountain lion resumed their journey to the kingdom on the Yakteree, she had no idea that one mountain lion had substituted himself for another.

"She soon noticed that her mountain lion attacked his prey with more relish. Before it had seemed a necessary evil, but now he seemed to enjoy it. He has been away from the civilizing influence of his kingdom for too long, she thought. When he caressed her she had to keep reminding him to retract his claws, and sometimes when she rose in the morning there were streaks of dried blood on her skin. Worst of all, she found herself lying alone at night, as the mountain lion would no longer hold her, but just roll over and go to sleep. As she lay awake, gazing at the stars and shivering, she tried to warm herself with memories of home with her parents and Trisky and Crumble Dee, her head cradled at her mother's breast.

"*He is merely weary from the journey,* she told herself, and for heaven's sake they were together all the time, which would be hard on any budding relationship. Her mountain lion would return to her. It was only a phase.

"Now, there are some who say that Maisy Bumble knew something was up. Perhaps not consciously, but somewhere, buried under all that wishful thinking, she knew that this was not her mountain lion. But she had been so lost and alone in the world that she could not bear to admit that her only companion was not himself, and so she clung fiercely to the memory of their early days. The scars on her skin and her heart would fade, she knew — these were hardships worth suffering. And as fortunes went, one could do much worse than to be queen of a mountain lion's kingdom on the Yakteree.

"One day they climbed up the side of a mountain, and at the top, glistening in the distance, she saw it — the kingdom on the Yakteree. Its castle's golden turrets gleamed in the sun; the sky was bluer there, the sun shone brighter, the clouds puffed up like *trompe l'oeil* ornaments on a Baroque palace's ceiling. In all those nights of listening to the mountain lion's tales of his youth as a prince in the kingdom on the Yakteree, she had never imagined anything so glorious. Even the mountain lion seemed to have recovered from his recent moodiness. Overcome by his kingdom's glow reflected in Maisy's eyes, he gazed at her tenderly.

"'You look just like your mother,' he sighed, drawing a paw against her cheek.

"'My — my mother?' Maisy turned to the mountain lion in sudden terror.

"'Your mother had that same glow of anticipation on the muddy banks of the lower delta of the

Daisymactawphaw River. How I longed to take her with me to my kingdom on the Yakteree, to sit beside me on a gilded throne. But your father would have none of it,' he shrugged, 'so I had to eat them both.'

"Maisy Bumble raced downhill, the mountain lion bounding after her. He would catch her and claw her open and taste the fresh young flesh he had been craving for so long. She was his — she had set her fortune with him, and now had to live up to her end of the bargain. He would have Maisy Bumble, one way or another.

"Maisy ran faster than she thought her aching legs could carry her, fleet as a jackal once more, until she slid over a patch of moldy leaves and tumbled into a crevasse, her ankle twisted beyond immediate use. She reached back for her slingshot while her other hand groped for a stone. The mountain lion pounced.

"And that was the end of Maisy Bumble."

If there was a moral to this story it eluded me, for, to the clitoris' consternation, its audience had fallen asleep somewhere on the road to the Yakteree. When I awoke, hair reeking of moldy carpet, the clitoris was gone.

Now I was in trouble.

Meredith would be arriving soon — she had just wrapped a show in Lisbon — and what would I tell her about Marie Bonaparte's clitoris? That it told me a story about a girl and a mountain lion that put me to sleep, and then took off? A clitoris doesn't just get up off its pin and walk out of its bell jar.

It couldn't have gone far. With no money — no pockets for money. No, it was probably hiding somewhere between my stacks of books. It was playing with me.

So I started looking on tiptoes, shining a flashlight between the book towers, being careful not to topple them and inadvertently squash the little bugger. I aimed it across the carpet, under the sink, between the shower stall and the refrigerator.

And when I came up empty I started talking to it, coaxing it to come out.

"I'm sorry I fell asleep," I pleaded. "I'd had a really busy day. It was a terrific story; I'd love to hear the rest. What happened to Maisy Bumble? Please?"

Dead silence. Meredith would arrive and see what I had done and curse my irresponsibility, throwing me out. I would lose my home, my shell. Aelian writes: "Hermit-crabs are born without a shell and select for themselves the shell that makes the best house for them to live in." And so it is with me. I was born shell-less, and have found in Meredith's shell the best house for me. It is warm in here, amid the clutter — my piles of books, her dismantled scrap metal — safe, a perfect fit. I will never give it up, will never leave. She cannot make me, no matter what sin I commit.

•

Marie Bonaparte's clitoris was moved three times. The third time it was actually stolen, only to be recovered by the infallible ratiocinations of the one and only Monsieur Dupin. He found it hiding in plain sight, as he did the purloined letter, which was hanging, as Poe recounts, "from a little brass knob just beneath the middle of the mantelpiece." Marie identifies this knob as the clitoris, and the purloined letter as the mother's penis, which the child imagines is castrated by the father during the primal scene. Dupin and Minister D—— are locked in an Oedipal struggle over the castrated mother/wife: the son convicts the father of stealing the letter, of sleeping with his beloved.

Bonaparte theorizes that Poe created the unflaggingly logical Dupin in order to stem fears of his own dwindling sanity. I have no such problems. No need to create a Master Detective. If I were mad, it would be obvious. You would know.

•

It is not as if a bit of genital has never gone missing before. Exhibit A (*objet a*): The Holy Foreskin of Jesus Christ our Lord and Savior. You have seen the paintings of the circumcision of the Baby Jesus, but have you seen his foreskin?

It is said that Mary Mother of God wore her son's foreskin in a locket around her neck, to be restored to Him on the Day of Judgment, so that he could appear before his Father as the Good Lord made him. Why didn't she let her son carry it with him? Well, we all know how children lose things.

And yet Mary passed before Judgment Day, leaving the Holy Foreskin to St. John. This according to St. Birgitta of Sweden; a variant of the tale, not supported by saintly revelation, has Mother Mary bequeathing it to Mary Magdalene, who surely knew from foreskins. From her it passed to the Apostles, and as the generations receded into the Dark Ages, so did the Foreskin.

We have no further record of the Holy Foreskin until the eighth century, when an angel bestowed it upon the Emperor Charlemagne as a sign of heavenly endorsement, either at his palace at Aix-la-Chapelle or while genuflecting at the Holy Sepulcher in Jerusalem. Charlemagne, knowing well the value of political gifts, regifted it to Pope Innocent III, who enshrined it in the Sancta Sanctorum next to the decapitated noggins of Peter and Paul and several shards of the True Cross.

Roman women privileged to glimpse the Holy Foreskin were enraptured by its heady fragrance, sweeter than honey, more delicate than silk. And there it rested, venerated but undisturbed, until the Sacking of Rome in May of 1527. So we might surmise a connection between the theft of the Holy Foreskin and the waning of the Middle Ages.

The German mercenary who stole the Foreskin made it thirty miles north to the village of Calcata, where he was swiftly imprisoned. Now displayed in the village's humble abbey, the Foreskin brought nothing but blessings: rain to the crops when the neighbors went dry, bountiful fertility to animal and man alike. The heady fragrance that had so enraptured the women of Rome drenched the very air the villagers breathed. A line of pilgrims waited patiently for miles outside the village's stone walls to genuflect before the Holy Foreskin, for which they would earn a decade's worth of Papal indulgence.

This, then, was the official Holy Foreskin. In 1856 the Charroux Abbey, southeast of Nantes, claimed to be in possession of the Foreskin given by the angel to Charlemagne. As, at various points, did the abbeys of Antwerp, Besançon, Bologna, Bruges, Compostela, Compiègne, Conques, Hildesheim, Le Puy, Nancy and Paris.

For women, the Holy Foreskin was a balm of unequalled salubrity: the Charroux Foreskin eased the discomforts of pregnancy; another cured the Queen of Sicily's intractable lumbago; and at one abbey the nuns were said to have been swept into unspeakable acts under the sway of this most seductive of relics. For women of faith, the Holy Foreskin had always had a provocative allure: St. Agnes of Blannbekin, who as a child had been overcome with tears on the anniversary of His

Circumcision for the distress inflicted on the Baby Jesus, could summon the Foreskin on her tongue, its ambrosial nectar now conveyed with the viscousness of egg white, and with a mere tap of her finger the Foreskin would slide down her throat, her body shuddering in convulsions of ecstatic communion. This according to Alphons Victor Müller, *De Praeputio Domini* (1907) Chapter XXXVII, via our old friend Felix Bryk.

By the turn of the last century, the Church was dealing with the dueling foreskins by excommunicating those who even spoke of its existence; in 1954, after a monk sought to put Calcata on a papally sanctioned pilgrim's progress, the punishment was either upped or modified (depending on how you look at it) to shunning. Vatican 2 removed the Day of the Holy Circumcision from the calendar, and yet Calcata continued to observe it, in defiance of all Papal ordinances.

And so the Calcata Foreskin remained, hidden in a shoebox in the back of the priest's closet, until it was stolen in 1983. The culprit is unknown: some accuse treasure-hunters, and many more the Vatican itself. And some suspect that the priest returned the Holy Foreskin to the Vatican, just to be rid of the whole damn business. And now it resides there, a shriveled snip of pinkish, bluish flesh, persisting in all opposition to assertions of its nonexistence.

Or so some say. For others say that Jesus met his Father intact once more, and that all the Holy Foreskins have been Holy Frauds.

So you see, Marie Bonaparte's clitoris could have gone anywhere. Abducted by the impresario of a museum of curiosities. Ingested by a Freudian thirsting for symbolism. Or just gone to seek its fortune, to tell its tale to ears more attentive than mine.

•

It could have gone to call on Monsieur Dupin, offering its services as a pint-sized Watson. It could have gone to Utrecht to apprentice with Melchior d'Hondecoeter, if it could only figure out how to pick up a paintbrush. It could have gone off with Felix Bryk to Ethiopia's Omo Bottego, where the Djangero cut off their sons' nipples so they won't look like women, or to Northern Transvaal, where the Bapedi stretch their daughters' inner labia until they dangle below the vulva, so that they resemble penises from far away. One tribe accuses nature of erasing the distinctions of sex; the other tries to erase such distinctions. In both, it is preferable to be a man.

•

For centuries it was believed that the hyena changed its sex once a year, a mistaken notion owing to the size of the female hyena's clitoris. Aesop recounts two fables: in the first, a female hyena is rejected by a fox because he can't discern her sex; in the second, a female hyena acquiesces to a male hyena's sexual overtures, telling him she'll return the favor soon enough.

Not all of Aesop is as child-friendly and morally edifying as "The Tortoise and the Hare," you know. Aelian, of the dolphin-boy love, takes the hyena's polymorphic perversity as zoological fact. But then he also avows the existence of gryphons and sea monsters and by his own admission didn't get out of Rome much. And Barnabas, in an epistle elaborating on Levitican dietary restrictions, insists that thou shalt not eat hyena, "because this animal changes its nature from year to year and becomes now male, now female." Eating hyena will make you "an adulterer or a corrupter of boys." Likewise, eating weasel is as sinful as fellatio, "for this animal conceives with its mouth."

There *are* animals that change their sex, polymorphic and perverse. The slipper limpet, for one. It's not for nothing that biologists named this American snail *Crepidula fornicata*. When one male limpet (they're all born male) comes of age, he attaches himself to a rock, or a ship's hull, and becomes female. Another male limpet soon gets on top of the first one, fertilizing the now-female limpet below. More male limpets pile on top of them to fertilize that bottom limpet, or become female themselves as the need arises, in a tower of as many as fourteen, fishermen's nuisances reproducing like — well, like slipper limpets. Once they've taken their place in the copulatory tower they never leave. They just fuck — if snails can be said to fuck — until they die. Their discarded shells choke the sea floor, altering the ecosystem and suffocating marine life. They wreak havoc in oyster bays, deviously inhibiting the aphrodisia of the harvest. You might conjecture that they're out to get us.

The *Labroides* fish have it all figured out. They make their home on coral reefs, living like Mormons, one male with six or so wives. When the male expires, or is removed from the family by a curious scientist, the biggest wife secretes a hormone that was suppressed by her mate and becomes the new husband. Or if the family is too successful reproduction-wise, one of the larger wives turns male and takes half the family with her.

The echiuroid worm *Bonellia* lives by the kind of situational sexuality observed in prisons and single-sex boarding schools. Without interference, its larva will mature into a female, but if the larva settles inside a female worm, it becomes a male parasite, fertilizing the host's eggs, which sounds pretty efficient and a nice twist on the whole Mormon-harem thing. As many as eighty-five of these male worms have been observed inside a single female.

And then there's the tapeworm, which grows innumerable sets of male and female sex organs and can go fuck itself, literally. How do you think they get so big? I once read about one that was over two hundred feet long and had more than 22,000 sex organs. Believe it or not.

Urban legends tell of women buying tapeworms through the mail in pursuit of an anorexic form, and I believe this is no legend. Men claim to hate a bag of bones, but watch their heads turn when the truly skeletal walks by. They can't help themselves; it's the oversexed parasite inside the anorexic that's beckoning them, those 22,000 voracious sex organs that have consumed her body.

And some protozoa have more than two sexes — eight in the single cell of the *Paramecium amelia*, ten in the single cell of the algae of the genus *Chlamydomonas*, although the latter can reproduce asexually as well. This, perhaps, is where we're headed, evolutionarily: beyond binary, or self-sufficiently alone.

•

Last night I dreamt that Marie Bonaparte's clitoris went in search of its rightful owner. If Jesus could be reunited with His Holy Foreskin, why not Marie Bonaparte? But the clitoris realized, after an expensive transatlantic red-eye on which it got little sleep, and a Google Map that terminated at a grave at Montparnasse, that it was too late. The clitoris sat on the stone and wept until dark when, shooed out by the groundskeeper, it repaired to a café for an absinthe, and then another. Steeling itself with liquid courage, it tried to attach itself to the passing *filles*, but its French had deteriorated in its years abroad, along with its powers of persuasion, and the women of Paris, inured as they are to the come-ons of *artistes de ramassage*, just walked on.

Out of money and hope, the clitoris hitched a ride in an Hermès handbag, which was snatched in the Tuileries and fenced at the flea market at Clignancourt to a tourist who took it for fake. It traveled with her south to an ancient Greek village, where the shouts of the fishermen echoed off the walls and the air tasted of brine and diesel and the calls of the seagulls reminded it of home. But the clitoris began to ponder whose home this really was, and eventually there was the awkward moment, the "What are you doing in my purse?" that could not be satisfactorily answered, and it was at this moment that I woke up.

But the clitoris was still dreaming.

•

It has been suggested that the word "clitoris" is derived from the Greek word *kleis*, meaning "key." The girl in the Grimm tale who cuts off her little finger to turn the lock of the cell imprisoning her seven brothers who have been turned into ravens — that's no little finger. And there goes Bluebeard's latest bride, alone in his damp, rambling castle, unlocking one chamber of secrets after another. No wonder Bluebeard flies into a rage when he gets home, for he has been rendered superfluous.

•

I still hear them at night, in my castle, her castle, without chambers, without doors: the breathing, the pounding, the gasps, the creaking joints of Meredith's bed. If I draw the covers down from over my head, I can watch them. We have no secrets, Meredith and I. No curtains. They are there every night with her, on her, a parade of the tall and the thin and the lank-haired, the photographers, sculptors, musicians, curators, professors. I close my eyes and let the ostinato thrust its way in, into my heart through my limbs to the vibrating tips of my fingers and toes, becoming one with the insistent ictus, its hellish tattoo pounding rhythmically into my brain.

It was Marie Bonaparte, in her book on Poe, who connected the heartbeat under the floorboards in "The Tell-Tale Heart" to the child overhearing her parents having sex. She is obsessed with the primal scene, having witnessed it so often between her wet nurse and the stable boy. It is from such memories that psychoanalysts are made.

Poe, being somewhat of a necrophiliac, probably had something else in mind.

•

You might be wondering what became of Meredith's cat. I was wondering that myself. I guess I was supposed to feed her — I'm sure Meredith gave me instructions, the organic chow from the pet store, not the supermarket Friskies. But what was I feeding, exactly? A plush toy, neutered for our amusement? Was it truly alive? Did it really have an appetite?

So I suppose I forgot to feed the cat. Was that such a crime? Don't cats have nine lives?

I must have heard her purring devolve into mewling, her enfeebled pleas, her last cries for mercy.

And then it was over.

People think dead things smell, but that's only for a little while. The odor passes with time, with the process of decomposition. And then it's as if there was never any life there at all.

But Malinka has not decomposed. She is right here, behind the stove.

She's remarkably well preserved. Look at this fur, dried to a jagged crisp. Those eyes forever open like a porcelain doll's. Those teeth, pointed and sharp, that mouth in permanent caterwaul. Touch her — go ahead. Poke her with your shoe.

She's become one with Rauschenberg's goat, Grünfeld's sheep-dog, Messager's sparrows: an honest-to-Ra mummy, like the beloved cats of Egypt.

The Ancient Egyptians were buried with their cats. Their warrior goddess Bastet, a cat. The Hindus have their monkey-god, the Egyptians their cat-god; you can tell a lot about a people by the animals they worship. Christianity is the only religion with the hubris to worship a man.

And yet the Egyptians honored their cats by killing them young, snapping their necks well before that first life was up, so they would be immortalized young and beautiful. It has always been this way. The spates of youthful suicides inspired by Werther and his successors. The Buddhist monks who slowly strangle themselves to death with a belt anchored in the lotus position. The rock stars who flamed out at 27. Would Jesus have such a following if he had been crucified wrinkled and balding, his flesh sagging off his bones? I understand this. I would not like to see Meredith past her prime.

•

They used to grind up mummies for pigment. Humans and cats. The flesh tones in a Delacroix? Mummy brown. Human remains on canvas, transformed into art, rendered immortal. When Edward Burnes-Jones found out that mummy brown was not just an evocative name he was so unnerved he buried the paint tube in his garden. Those Pre-Raphaelites, so naïve.

It was unstable, this mummy brown. The bits of animal fat interacted irregularly, unpredictably, with other pigments. Over time mummy brown became dull and cracked, prematurely aging its subjects — "The Mummy's Revenge," one might call it. In the antiquarian journal *Notes and Queries,* F. G. Stephens recounts the strange case of William Hilton the Younger's *Sir Calapine Rescuing Serena,* in which one eye of Spenser's much-imperiled maiden, painted with this mummy brown, began to drift down her cheek, until someone at the National Gallery had the good sense to turn the painting upside down until the eye slid back to its place of origin.

I thumb through my book of Dutch still lifes, so rich in umber, and wonder which ones used mummy brown. Death in a paintbrush.

•

She's getting away with murder. One hears this all the time. But one never actually means murder.

On a late-summer's day in 1925 while on a pleasant drive through the countryside, one Madame Guillaume Lefebvre, matriarch of one of Northern France's wealthiest families, shot her daughter-in-law in cold blood. Her son was behind the wheel. The victim was six months pregnant with what would have been Madame Lefebvre's first grandchild. At trial she showed no remorse, and was sentenced to death. Intrigued by this sensational case, so pregnant with Freudian symbolism, Marie Bonaparte took on *la meurtrière notoire* as her first jailhouse patient. Madame Lefebvre remained unrepentant, insisting she was doing God's will, that she had put down her daughter-in-law as one "kills a wild animal."

Like a wild animal. Meredith is like a wild animal, footloose and untethered. She has gone to South America on the back of a Venezuelan's motorcycle. She is speaking in tongues with the Maori, drinking their firewater and hallucinating visions of madness. She is in a Tuscan village dancing in a vat of grapes, their rosy flesh bursting like blood vessels.

In Meredith's absence I have been sketching plans for an installation, for you cannot be around such work without thinking, *I could do this myself.* On the floor I will put a map of the world, with pins marking every place Meredith has been. And locked in a cage, at the center of the map, will be Meredith. My wild animal.

•

Based on Bonaparte's testimony that the prisoner suffered from an Electra complex, having seen in her pregnant daughter-in-law her own pregnant mother and rival for her father's affections, Madame Lefebvre's sentence was commuted to life. And it was with this victory that Bonaparte began her campaign against the death penalty, culminating in her visits to Caryl Chessman in San Quentin.

Chessman had been convicted of being the Red Light Bandit, terror of Los Angeles lovers' lanes, so-called because he would place a policeman's red light on top of his car and, impersonating an officer, shine a flashlight (of obvious phallic import) into the womb of the couple's automobile. On at least two occasions he dragged the distaff half of the couple away from the car. On one of these occasions he forced 17-year-old Mary Alice Meza to fellate him.

He was a Freudian dream of a patient. Even as a boy he was no stranger to lovers' lanes. According to his own account in his 1954 memoir *Cell 2455 Death Row,* he once came upon a couple in the throes of intercourse in the backseat of a car. The woman's wailing young daughter was struggling to crawl over the front seat, only to be smacked down by the man for so rudely interrupting his exertions. And so he shot the man, shot him with his little BB gun. The original primal scene.

He had to be taunted into sex — Virginia in the car, it was always a car, what was wrong with him, didn't he want her? And then after his first, confiding her first, with her father, it was always her father. And sometimes he would leap out of that car and run away, run from these women who wanted him so, wanted him to exorcise their own primal scene, run from his memory of the couple in the backseat, the crying child in the front.

"The dialectics of psychopathy are subtle and romantic indeed," he wrote, and romance is perhaps what Bonaparte saw in Chessman's struggle, the hardened criminal who wrote well and quoted even better (Dr. Johnson and Swinburne, as well as Machiavelli and Nietzsche). Here they are in a 1960 wire service snapshot, hands clasped at the corner of a table. The hawk-like Chessman looms over the now diminutive princess, as if she were weighed down by an invisible crown. Although her hand is on top of his, it looks like he is visiting her. She could be his grandmother, the prison a nursing home.

What did she see in him? Was it merely a psychoanalyst's interest in a patient unable to recover from the primal scene, compelled to revisit it again and again? Did she see herself sitting across the table, there but for the grace of God go I? Was she the one who could not get past that first memory, the nurse and the stable boy, both shrouded and heightened by narcotic fog?

Chessman wrote that exploding cyanide eggs smell like peach blossoms, and it occurs to me here that I have never seen a peach blossom, much less smelled one.

As for Mary Alice Meza, she went mad. Her prison a mental institution, committed for life.

•

I once saw a woman standing on the corner, what we used to call a bag lady when we called their male counterparts bums, although she pushed no shopping cart stuffed with plastic bags. She was dressed in scraps from the garbage, frayed woven slip-ons, her skirt dragging on the sidewalk. Her skin was marked with short red cuts. She was taking scissors to her face — cuticle scissors, I think — and making tiny incisions, muttering to herself.

A policeman came by, asking her to come with him. She was putting up a real fuss. No one wants to go to the asylum. No woman is that mad.

•

"Marie Bonaparte had her clitoris moved three times."

I look up from the biography I've been leafing through on the New Releases table. His voice, rumbling and confident, draws me upward. His name is Miles and it suits him, the way his lanky frame looms over me like a construction crane about to scoop me up. His concerned gray eyes gaze down only slightly, so as not to tilt his head and let tumble a long, precious lock of silky blond hair, combed back precariously over a hairline poised for recession.

I recognize him from Meredith's party, one of the men in her circle, the one without a cigarette, the one who seemed to be above it all, breathing his own rarified air. He teaches women's studies and knows a lot about Marie Bonaparte. "Did you know Aristide Briande was her lover? That her husband was, we suspect, rather homosexual?" He hints that he has known the biographer intimately.

There ensues a conversation I can't recall, so overwhelmed am I. A coffee in the co-op café, although he abstains from coffee, and alcohol, and all drugs, prescription or otherwise, and I think to myself, a man like this never gets sick.

As he rises from the table I am taken by the way he moves, not with the authority of a man in whom height breeds confidence or the apologetic posture of a man who wishes he did not stick out quite so much. No, he moves like a jungle cat, a magnificent beast of prey, and yet he is somehow circumspect, as if he is being followed. He takes my hand, as if to allay my suspicions.

He lives in that new glass tower by the pier. "It's just a sublet," he says, by way of apology. Inside it is as I had imagined such an apartment would be: immaculate and dustless, the strangely few books shelved by the graduated colors of their spines, sliding closet doors concealing all manner of domestic horrors. I make a crack about it all being a little Patrick Bateman and he says, "Who?"

And yet the natural world encroaches as if sprouting through the poured concrete floor, like a return of the repressed: in the decorative fireplace a percolating fish tank; on the round glass coffee table a labyrinth of stones, almost hypnotic; above the bed's hard iron bars a canopy of branches, suspended from the ceiling by no discernible means.

In the mirror of an antique dresser his naked body embraces mine, but I am distracted by the arrangement before me: three leather-bound volumes, stacked just so and crowned with a skull I assure myself is plastic; beside it a conch shell, howling, a pair of candlesticks, a ukulele, the entire assemblage twisted with a rope of ivy. "Vanitas," he whispers. "I've always had a weakness for Dutch still lifes."

He touches me as if he is both discovering my body and has known me all my life. He envelopes me like an actual envelope, folds me in, kisses me like it means everything.

He pulls and pushes me like a rag doll, and I just go with it, watching that forelock drop low over his face and down to his chin like filaments of cornsilk. He flips me over and pushes me onto all fours with one hard palm against my spine, and then silence. I hear a salivary lump expel from his lips and plummet, from his great height, on a long mucosal string, in the extended seconds of a long intake of breath. And I think about this as he comes, hollering.

In bed we talk admiringly of Gloria Steinem's long fingers and Naomi Wolf's voluminous hair. Of first and second and third-wave, of riot grrrls and flappers and suffragettes. He seems inordinately burdened by the fate of Mary Alice Meza, deeply troubled by the rising accusations of rape on college campuses. He is up on every challenge to Roe v. Wade, every lawsuit for equal pay, every asylum seeker fleeing ritual mutilation in Africa. He is particularly enamored of the post-Lacanian French feminists and their celebration of a pleasure that men can never know, thanks to the extra pair of lips between their legs, rubbing together in a state of perpetual *jouissance*, and when I laugh at this absurdity he silences me with a finger at my lips. With the index and thumb of his other hand he reaches down and seals those second lips shut.

He refuses my number. We will meet again at the co-op bookstore, at the New Releases table, and while I wait for him I will read that entire 600-page biography of Marie Bonaparte, standing. But he comes, and he comes, always from behind, always the pause for that long drip, that lump of spit.

He has stopped using condoms and I don't ask him to put one on. This gives me leverage, I think, over the women who do.

Afterwards he holds me, a once-lost letter now secure in its envelope. We stay up talking late into the night — for he also appears to have little need for sleep — about this art show and that new study and all the culture our voracious appetites have consumed. The night has suspended our sense of time, or at least mine, and so we never speak of our past, or our future, for these would require a paradigmatic shift out of this precious eternal present. As we stand naked in the kitchen eating spelt toast smeared with avocado, I realize I know nothing about him — where he's from, whether he has siblings or kids, tucked away in one of those nice Victorians across town with a woman with whom he used to stand naked in the kitchen eating spelt toast smeared with avocado.

He plies me with questions, sweet and inconsequential, taking careful note of my answers, it seems, with his eyes. Where in the world would I most like to go? How would I define a perfect life? A perfect day? He asks me who my perfect man would be and I say, teasing, "you." I ask him and he says she'd be a combination of Germaine Greer, Patti Smith and some little girl from the Disney Channel. When I laugh at this he looks, for one brief, unguarded moment, as if he might cry.

In the morning I stumble out of the shower and scrounge under the dustless bed for last night's underwear, stopping to admire that physical perfection, now sound asleep, and I think, more profoundly, "you." I wash last night's dishes and stand on my tiptoes in the foolish hope that those tidy cabinets above the sink might hide an errant teabag.

And then he is behind me again, like a phantom, stopping my breath, stopping time. And when he is finished, those two fingers again like a vise, sealing me shut. He somehow pulls my panties back up from my ankles without the elastic ever touching my legs. And it occurs to me that such a trick requires a great deal of practice.

"What is it, exactly, that you do?" he asks me one night, while tracing a constellation of freckles under my left ribs.

He laughs when I tell him, as if that can't possibly be a real job.

"Aside from the clean up it's not so bad. The horses and cattle are the worst, and the pigs. You must have seen Meredith's thing with the pigs."

"Meredith?"

"My roommate?"

He stares at me as if I'm speaking gibberish.

"That's how we met. The pig room. It was a very big deal. A whole gallery of pigs, and there she was, naked, smack in the middle, spooning with them."

"How did you keep them from getting up?"

"Drugs. Animals don't have the fortitude of performance artists, you know. It's discipline that animals lack, discipline that keeps them down on the farm."

He laughs with a hearty convulsion that seems to radiate up from his toes, and rolls on top of me again.

•

I've found a clipping of Meredith resting naked with the pigs, laid end to end across the gallery in an undulating surface of pig lumps into which she curved her curves, fetal and silent.

This was the first in a series that Meredith had planned. There was to be a lying down with turtles, with bumblebees, and finally in a fish tank, in scuba gear. "Meredith sleeps with the fishes," the headline would have said.

I had been pulling for Fürst and Tanaka's termite colony, an easily tended labyrinth modeled on a 1948 Ford Motor plant, easily tended because once the termites died they, like auto workers, were not replaced. But Skip got that one; I got the pigs. Meredith's a pain in the ass, the boss said, and Skip's got no people skills.

And let me tell you what a pain in the ass. First, she made her wranglers wear overalls. Fucking denim overalls, with straw poking out of the back pockets like "Hee Haw." And she was always late, like hours, but when you figured on sleeping in she'd be on time and hell hath no wrath.

Then there was the pigs' diet. To control their emissions, their slop had to be mixed specially, low fiber and high fat. Meredith preferred her pigs constipated.

The diet began to sicken the pigs. The vet demanded the removal of the ailing pigs, but Meredith refused. One by one each pig turned blue, choking on its distended colon. And Meredith continued to lie there naked among them, once sleeping, now dead.

Of course I am talking about the pigs.

•

Marie Bonaparte might have pointed out that "Meredith" has *merde* in it. Shit. Also "death," homophonically. She would have found that pregnant with meaning. The toilet-training child, fascinated with her feces, who must renounce her attachment to her mother, along with the phallic clitoris, on the road to sexual maturity. One exchanges the shit instinct for the death instinct, for a thousand *petites morts*.

The French make it sound so tragic.

•

After the first weeks Miles' appearances at the bookstore become less frequent. The furtive dance of his movements has taken on new meaning, as if he is always looking over his shoulder, and as I eye the other women eyeing us I wonder if they also share secrets with him, if they rendezvous downstairs in natural history or upstairs among the oversized art books.

He is seeing others, I can tell, because he rubs me too hard, as if it will hasten the obligatory ladies-first orgasm. As he pushes into me he turns his head from side to side as if I am Medusa, as if I have a head of snakes, as if meeting my gaze will turn him to stone.

There is no envelope now, no pillow talk, no avocado on toast. He gets dressed, has somewhere to go. He is going to see Meredith, I know it. I push him against his apartment door, unzip his pants, take him in my mouth.

His penis, flaccid, is barely there, dwarfed by pendulous testicles that hang far below, the swollen left straining as if it might break through its sack and roll onto the floor. But in my mouth it becomes massive, as if three normal-guy dicks had been rolled into one, and I hone that mass in my mouth, the mass that curls on the end like an upside-down question mark, the fist-shape he likes to press hard against my cervix. And when it shrinks I bring it back to size, over and over again, my jaw aching, my lips on fire, refusing to let go, to let him go. It is interminable, this ebb and flow that refuses to actually flow. And then he takes that question mark in hand, rubs it rapidly, and it exclamation points into my mouth.

•

Marie Bonaparte's clitoris moved three times.

To 30 B.C. Alexandria, where it watched a 39-year-old Cleopatra feed herself to the asp. To 1580 Vitry-le-François, where Marie Germain had grown a heavy beard and was now living, in full but alone, as a man. To 1950s Tangier, where it trawled for young boys with William Burroughs and was left mercifully unmolested.

To the haunted forest of Hoia-Baciu, to commune with the ghosts of murdered Romanian peasants trapped within its twisted arbors. To Japan's Aokigahara, the Forest of Suicides where no birds sing and park rangers rock-paper-scissors to avoid spending the night with the corpses. To the Socotra Archipelago, where the dragon's blood trees grow like umbrellas and the pomegranates are out of this world.

To a shoebox in the back of a priest's closet. To a blue Tiffany box wrapped by an angel. To the back of St. Agnes' throat, and boy, she didn't know what hit her.

•

Miles and I meet one last time for an actual date, our first after all these weeks of furtiveness. There's a piece he wants to see at the museum, a recreation of one of the leather bar scenes in *Cruising* enacted by cocker spaniels. "It's my favorite movie," he says.

I worked on this one, dressing up the dogs in leather doggie jackets and cute little biker caps. Like a viral pet video, the piece is adorable and stupid at the same time. All, that is, except for the taxidermied tableau in the middle. A dog lies in a sling, legs in the air, as naked as a dog can be, while another dog, standing on hindquarters clad in chaps and motorcycle boots, shoves his paw up the dog's ass; a third dog proffers the standing dog a can of Crisco like Oliver Twist with his gruel bowl. The entire thing is mechanized, the paw twisting as it slides inside and out, the mouth of the dog in the sling frozen in an eternal howl. Miles stands there, as if contemplating a sculpture. "Who was that artist who tied a dog to a tree and shot him in the head?" he asks.

Back at his place he flips me over, spits, pushes my body flat against the mattress. The spit has a new target. At first I joke that he's too big for that, but he doesn't seem to hear me. He presses my hands down hard, pins my legs with the weight of his own. I cry out, beg him to stop, tell him he's hurting me, as he makes his way in, pressing that awful question mark into me with nothing but spit, and it occurs to me, suffering the expert navigation of his maneuvers as he shifts his angle by fractional degrees each excruciating millimeter to accommodate that massive tip, that this has also required a great deal of practice. And I wonder, what would Meredith do? What would Meredith do if she felt her backside being torn open by a Rodin fist, no longer chucked under the chin in contemplation but driven to action, to terror, to obliteration? Would her screams have been louder? And then I remember that such things do not happen to women like Meredith.

On the toilet I try to wipe off the blood and semen. It seems an endless slurry.

•

A storm is brewing. There's a goddamn hound braying outside my window. The howls of a junkyard dog, chained to barbed wire to scare off intruders and now forgotten, and the storm is coming and it has no defense. But there is no junkyard, perhaps no dog.

•

Aelian tells of the dog-headed men of Aithiopia, the Kynokephaloi, who wear leather and walk on their hind legs, catch gazelles and antelopes for dinner by outrunning them, and shred their meat into bits that they cook in the hot sun, for they don't yet know fire. Nor do they know speech; they understand the human tongue, but can only respond in deafening shrieks.

They are a peaceful people, and will never harm a man. Their babies will feed at a woman's breast, as if she were their own mother.

There is me, there I am, there we are. Romulus to the she-wolf. Stuffed with sawdust and stuffed into a tire on a ramp at the Guggenheim. A little girl is pointing at me, but her parents hurry her away.

•

Have you ever noticed the way swallows scatter helter-skelter in the moments before a storm, as if unsure of the safest direction to go?

The clouds are darkening, thickening, looming lower, suffering the gravitational pull of the earth. They are bearing down on us, me and that braying junkyard dog. They will invade our lungs, they will suffocate us, and the dog knows. He is warning me before it's too late.

•

The slides flash before me like bursts of lightening.

In this one, two spaniels have collapsed after a long afternoon's hunt, dead birds laid out before them. They lie on top of one another, the one above with lids in mid-droop — but the one below is alert, grinning, eyeing his kill and greedy for more.

In this one, three dogs have wandered into a placid still life. A greyhound sniffs at a rabbit hanging from the ceiling, while two foxhounds eye the pile of dead birds on the table. A rooster pokes his head out of that wicker basket, its beak thrust open in mid-cock-a-doodle, taunting them: "I'm not dead yet."

In this one, a stray dog has leapt into another precisely composed still life, knocking it to the ground. He hungrily tears into the raw shank of a cow while the house spaniel, liberated by a chaos he could never himself incite, gnaws gratefully on the end of sausage, rubbery and twisted like the intestine it once was. A cat eyes the spilled fruit and shattered porcelain with an expression that is unmistakable: "Ooh, I'm gonna tell…."

The cat sees everything. The cat cannot lie.

•

Mummified to a crisp, Malinka's heart still beats. At least I think it's her heart. Or is it mine, in the dark, a tenacious metronome in fierce counterpoint against the chaotic rhythms of the storm?

No, it is the cat's revenge. I hated that cat, neutered, good for nothing. What Meredith did to her. I relieved her of her misery. The beautiful ones are always miserable.

Malinka's stilled heart beats, still beats, like the beat-beat-beat of the tom-tom. Keeps me up at night, keeps me from dreaming. Or does it keep me dreaming?

•

I have long suspected that the culprit here is a failure of imagination.

The culprit in what? you ask.

Well, there are various crimes that may or may not have been committed. The disappearance, or theft, of Marie Bonaparte's clitoris. The not small matter of Meredith, who should be home by now. That thumping under the floorboards, amplified in solitude.

While Meredith has been away I have been tinkering with her latest installation, a Skinner Box employing her birds. Animal testing, you might call it. Every time I see one of those "not tested on animals" claims on a bottle of shampoo I have to laugh, because what has not been tested on animals? What was Skinner doing with his box or Pavlov with his dog? How many boons to humanity derive from experiments on animals? Our IQ tests, our methods of social conditioning. Our lives have been tested on animals.

Meredith's box has a choice of three levers. One lever feeds the bird, one does nothing, and the third issues an electrical shock that kills the bird instantly. The surviving bird is either smart enough to feed itself continuously or incurious enough not to try the third lever. Curiosity killed the bird, as it were.

I have suggested to Meredith that the "correct" lever change with each attempt, rendering the bird's powers of intelligence, such as they are, moot. We call this piece *We Never Learn*. The box appears Skinner, but it tests only luck. Meredith says it's cruel.

When a bird is electrocuted, the bottom of the box drops out, like the trapdoor under a hanged man, the corpse dumped into a clear plastic bin below. A door ushers in the unwitting entrance of the next bird. This, anyway, is the plan as I've diagrammed it. For now the birds lie on the floor, an unavoidable nuisance. It's just not the priority right now. Cleaning up Meredith's birds.

•

Meredith is coming home today. I got a postcard.

Just a moment, I have it somewhere around here.

All the places she's been! Somalia, Tangier, haunted forests and exotic archipelagos.

I have to tidy up for her. Don't want her to think I've let the place go. Some of the droppings have hardened and will require a razor blade and disinfectant. I should wash the sheets. Straighten the furniture. Pick up the birds.

•

Marie Bonaparte's clitoris is coming home today. I got a postcard.

Quite the adventure it's had! Ancient Alexandria, Aix-la-Chapelle, seventeenth-century Utrecht and Death Row San Quentin. But it says it has tired of wandering. That it's time to come home, to stop dreaming.

I dream of Meredith with the light brown hair. I've got some of it. All of it.

I will ask the clitoris, did it dream of Marie?

ACKNOWLEDGMENTS

I am indebted to the following:

The Dutch still life room at
the Metropolitan Museum of Art

The New York Public Library

The New York Society Library

33 Officina Creativa;
my fellow residents John Downing Bonafede,
Hyojin Jeong and Millie Schwier;
Claudia Ferrini; and Renato Vivaldi Tesser

The Edward F. Albee Foundation

Célia Bertin's *Marie Bonaparte, a Life*

Karl Steel's *How to Make a Human:
Animals and Violence in the Middle Ages*

Deena Drewis

Lisa Grubka

Jon Roemer

Justin Waldstein

ABOUT THE AUTHOR

Ann Lewinson's fiction has appeared in *Agni, Hayden's Ferry Review,* MoMA PS1's Special Projects Writers' Series and other places. A 2014 fellow at the Edward F. Albee Foundation, she is also a playwright, journalist and film critic who has reviewed movies for *ARTnews, The Boston Phoenix, The Hartford Advocate* and *The Kansas City Star.* She lives in New York.

Made in the USA
San Bernardino, CA
19 November 2019

60138682R00066